My son sleeps so soundly. Over his bed, five license plates are hung, the last four from Quebec, the first from Wisconsin. Five years ago, when he was six months old, we left to take a bad job in Montreal, where I was born but had never visited. My parents had brought me to the U.S. when I was six months old. Canada was at war, America was neutral. America meant opportunity, freedom; Montreal meant ghettos, and insults. And so, loving our children, we murder them. Following the sun, the dollars, the peace-of-mind, we blind ourselves. Better to be a professor's son than a salesman's son – better a thousand times, I think – better to ski than to feed the mordant hounds, better to swim at a summer cottage than debase yourself in the septic mud. But what do these license plates mean? Endurance? Exile, cunning? Where will we all wind up, and how?

A North American Education

A book of short fiction

by Clark Blaise

PaperJacks

A division of General Publishing Co. Limited
Don Mills, Ontario

Some of these stories have been previously published in the following periodicals: *Fiddlehead, Shenandoah, Tri-Quarterly, Florida Quarterly,* and *Tamarack*.

Published in PaperJacks 1974
Reprinted by arrangement with
Doubleday Canada Limited.

ISBN 0-7737-7055-0
Printed in Canada

For My Parents

Contents

Contents

The Montreal
Stories

So we never live, but we hope to live;
and, as we are always preparing to be happy,
it is inevitable we should never be so.

Blaise Pascal

Pensées

A Class of New
Canadians

Norman Dyer hurried down Sherbrooke
Street, collar turned against the snow. "Superb!" he muttered, passing a basement gallery next to a French bookstore. Bleached and tanned women in furs dashed from
hotel lobbies into waiting cabs. Even the neon clutter of
the side streets and the honks of slithering taxis seemed
remote tonight through the peaceful snow. *Superb*, he
thought again, waiting for a light and backing from a
slushy curb: a word reserved for wines, cigars, and delicate sauces; he was feeling superb this evening. After
eighteen months in Montreal, he still found himself
freshly impressed by everything he saw. He was proud
of himself for having steered his life north, even for
jobs that were menial by standards he could have demanded. Great just being here no matter what they
paid, looking at these buildings, these faces, and hearing
all the languages. He was learning to be insulted by simple bad taste, wherever he encountered it.

Since leaving graduate school and coming to Montreal, he had sampled every ethnic restaurant downtown and in the old city, plus a few Levantine places out in Outremont. He had worked on conversational French and mastered much of the local dialect, done reviews for local papers, translated French-Canadian poets for Toronto quarterlies, and tweaked his colleagues for not sympathizing enough with Quebec separatism. He attended French performances of plays he had ignored in English, and kept a small but elegant apartment near a colony of *émigré* Russians just off Park Avenue. Since coming to Montreal he'd witnessed a hold-up, watched a murder, and seen several riots. When stopped on the street for directions, he would answer in French or accented English. To live this well and travel each long academic summer, he held two jobs. He had no intention of returning to the States. In fact, he had begun to think of himself as a semi-permanent, semi-political exile.

Now, stopped again a few blocks farther, he studied the window of Holt-Renfrew's exclusive men's shop. Incredible, he thought, the authority of simple good taste. Double-breasted chalk-striped suits he would never dare to buy. Knitted sweaters, and fifty-dollar shoes. One tanned mannequin was decked out in a brash checkered sportscoat with a burgundy vest and dashing ascot. Not a price tag under three hundred dollars. Unlike food, drink, cinema, and literature, clothing had never really involved him. Someday, he now realized, it would. Dyer's clothes, thus far, had all been bought in a chain department store. He was a walking violation of American law, clad shoes to scarf in Egyptian cottons, Polish leathers, and woolens from the People's Republic of China.

He had no time for dinner tonight; this was Wednesday, a day of lectures at one university, and then an evening course in English as a Foreign Language at McGill, beginning at six. He would eat afterwards.

Besides the money, he had kept this second job because it flattered him. There was to Dyer something fiercely elemental, almost existential, about teaching both his language and his literature in a foreign country —like Joyce in Trieste, Isherwood and Nabokov in Berlin, Beckett in Paris. Also it was necessary for his students. It was the first time in his life that he had done something socially useful. What difference did it make that the job was beneath him, a recent Ph.D., while most of his colleagues in the evening school at McGill were idle housewives and bachelor civil servants? It didn't matter, even, that this job was a perversion of all the sentiments he held as a progressive young teacher. He was a god two evenings a week, sometimes suffering and fatigued, but nevertheless an omniscient, benevolent god. His students were silent, ignorant, and dedicated to learning English. No discussions, no demonstrations, no dialogue.

I love them, he thought. They need me.

He entered the room, pocketed his cap and ear muffs, and dropped his briefcase on the podium. Two girls smiled good evening.

They love me, he thought, taking off his boots and hanging up his coat; I'm not like their English-speaking bosses.

I love myself, he thought with amazement even while conducting a drill on word order. I love myself for tramping down Sherbrooke Street in zero weather just to help them with noun clauses. I love myself standing behind this podium and showing Gilles Carrier and Claude Veilleux the difference between the past continuous and the simple past; or the sultry Armenian girl with the bewitching half-glasses that "put on" is not the same as "take on"; or telling the dashing Mr. Miguel Mayor, late of Madrid, that simple futurity can be expressed in four different ways, at least.

This is what mastery is like, he thought. Being superb in one's chosen field, not merely in one's mother tongue. A respected performer in the lecture halls of the major universities, equipped by twenty years' research in the remotest libraries, and slowly giving it back to those who must have it. Dishing it out suavely, even wittily. Being a legend. Being loved and a little feared.

"Yes, Mrs. David?"

A *sabra:* freckled, reddish hair, looking like a British model, speaks with a nifty British accent, and loves me.

"No," he smiled, "*I were* is not correct except in the present subjunctive, which you haven't studied yet."

The first hour's bell rang. The students closed their books for the intermission. Dyer put his away, then noticed a page of his Faulkner lecture from the afternoon class. *Absalom, Absalom!* his favorite.

"Can anyone here tell me what the *impregnable citadel of his passive rectitude* means?"

"What, sir?" asked Mr. Vassilopoulos, ready to copy.

"What about *the presbyterian and lugubrious efflu-*

vium of his passive vindictiveness?" A few girls giggled.
"O.K.," said Dyer, "take your break."

In the halls of McGill they broke into the usual
groups. French-Canadians and South Americans into
two large circles, then the Greeks, Germans, Spanish,
and French into smaller groups. The patterns interested
Dyer. Madrid Spaniards and Parisian French always
spoke English with their New World co-linguals. The
Middle Europeans spoke German together, not Russian,
preferring one occupier to the other. Two Israeli men
went off alone. Dyer decided to join them for the break.

Not *sabras*, Dyer concluded, not like Mrs. David. The
shorter one, dark and wavy-haired, held his cigarette
like a violin bow. The other, Mr. Weinrot, was tall and
pot-bellied, with a ruddy face and thick stubby fingers.
Something about him suggested truck-driving, perhaps
of beer, maybe in Germany. Neither one, he decided,
could supply the name of a good Israeli restaurant.

"This is really hard, you know?" said Weinrot.

"Why?"

"I think it's because I'm not speaking much of English at my job."

"French?" asked Dyer.

"French? Pah! All the time Hebrew, sometimes German, sometimes little Polish. Crazy thing, eh? How long
you think they let me speak Hebrew if I'm working in
America?"

"Depends on where you're working," he said.

"Hell, I'm working for the Canadian government,
what you think? Plant I work in—I'm engineer, see—

[7]

makes boilers for the turbines going up North. Look. When I'm leaving Israel I go first to Italy. Right away-bamm I'm working in Italy I'm speaking Italian like a native. Passing for a native."

"A native Jew," said his dark-haired friend.

"Listen to him. So in Rome they think I'm from Tyrol—that's still native, eh? So I speak Russian and German and Italian like a Jew. My Hebrew is bad, I admit it, but it's a lousy language anyway. Nobody likes it. French I understand but English I'm talking like a bum. Arabic I know five dialects. Danish fluent. So what's the matter I can't learn English?"

"It'll come, don't worry," Dyer smiled. *Don't worry, my son;* he wanted to pat him on the arm. "Anyway, that's what makes Canada so appealing. Here they don't force you."

"What's this *appealing*? Means nice? Look, my friend, keep it, eh? Two years in a country I don't learn the language means it isn't a country."

"Come on," said Dyer. "Neither does forcing you."

"Let me tell you a story why I come to Canada. Then you tell me if I was wrong, O.K.?"

"Certainly," said Dyer, flattered.

In Italy, Weinrot told him, he had lost his job to a Communist union. He left Italy for Denmark and opened up an Israeli restaurant with five other friends. Then the six Israelis decided to rent a bigger apartment downtown near the restaurant. They found a perfect nine-room place for two thousand kroner a month, not bad shared six ways. Next day the landlord told them the deal was off. "You tell me why," Weinrot demanded.

No Jews? Dyer wondered. "He wanted more rent," he finally said.

"More—yóu kidding? More we expected. *Less* we didn't expect. A couple with eight kids is showing up after we're gone and the law in Denmark says a man has a right to a room for each kid plus a hundred kroner knocked off the rent for each kid. What you think of that? So a guy who comes in *after* us gets a nine-room place for a thousand kroner *less*. Law says no way a bachelor can get a place ahead of a family, and bachelors pay twice as much."

Dyer waited, then asked, "So?"

"So, I make up my mind the world is full of communismus, just like Israel. So I take out applications next day for Australia, South Africa, U.S.A., and Canada. Canada says come right away, so I go. Should have waited for South Africa."

"How could you?" Dyer cried. "What's wrong with you anyway? South Africa is fascist. Australia is racist."

The bell rang, and the Israelis, with Dyer, began walking to the room.

"What I was wondering, then," said Mr. Weinrot, ignoring Dyer's outburst, "was if my English is good enough to be working in the United States. You're American, aren't you?"

It was a question Dyer had often avoided in Europe, but had rarely been asked in Montreal. "Yes," he admitted, "your English is probably good enough for the States or South Africa, whichever one wants you first."

He hurried ahead to the room, feeling that he had let Montreal down. He wanted to turn and shout to Weinrot and to all the others that Montreal was the greatest city on the continent, if only they knew it as well as he did. If they'd just break out of their little ghettos.

At the door, the Armenian girl with the half-glasses caught his arm. She was standing with Mrs. David and Miss Parizeau, a jolly French-Canadian girl that Dyer had been thinking of asking out.

"Please, sir," she said, looking at him over the tops of her tiny glasses, "what I was asking earlier—*put on*—I heard on the television. A man said *You are putting me on* and everybody laughed. I think it was supposed to be funny but *put on* we learned means get dressed, no?"

"Ah—*don't put me on*," Dyer laughed.

"I yaven't erd it neither," said Miss Parizeau.

"To put some*body* on means to make a fool of him. To put some*thing* on is to wear it. O.K.?" He gave examples.

"Ah, now I know," said Miss Parizeau. "Like bullshitting somebody. Is it the same?"

"Ah, yes," he said, smiling. French-Canadians were like children learning the language. "Your example isn't considered polite. 'Put on' is very common now in the States."

"Then maybe," said Miss Parizeau, "we'll ave it ere in twenty years." The Armenian giggled.

"No—I've heard it here just as often," Dyer protested, but the girls had already entered the room.

He began the second hour with a smile which slowly soured as he thought of the Israelis. America's anticommunism was bad enough, but it was worse hearing it echoed by immigrants, by Jews, here in Montreal. Wasn't there a psychological type who chose Canada over South Africa? Or was it just a matter of visas and slow adjustment? Did Johannesburg lose its Greeks, and Melbourne its Italians, the way Dyer's students were always leaving Montreal?

And after class when Dyer was again feeling content and thinking of approaching one of the Israelis for a restaurant tip, there came the flood of small requests: should Mrs. Papadopoulos go into a more advanced course; could Mr. Perez miss a week for an interview in Toronto; could Mr. Giguère, who spoke English perfectly, have a harder book; Mr. Coté an easier one?

Then as he packed his briefcase in the empty room, Miguel Mayor, the vain and impeccable Spaniard, came forward from the hallway.

"Sir," he began, walking stiffly, ready to bow or salute. He wore a loud gray checkered sportscoat this evening, blue shirt, and matching ascot-handkerchief, slightly mauve. He must have shaved just before class, Dyer noticed, for two fresh daubs of antiseptic cream stood out on his jaw, just under his earlobe.

"I have been wanting to ask *you* something, as a matter of fact," said Dyer. "Do you know any good Spanish restaurants I might try tonight?"

"There are not any good Spanish restaurants in Montreal," he said. He stepped closer. "Sir?"

"What's on your mind, then?"

"Please—have you the time to look on a letter for me?"

He laid the letter on the podium.

"Look *over* a letter," said Dyer. "What is it for?"

"I have applied," he began, stopping to emphasize the present perfect construction, "for a job in Cleveland, Ohio, and I want to know if my letter will be good. Will an American, I mean—"

"Why are you going there?"

"It is a good job."

"But Cleveland—"

"They have a blackman mayor, I have read. But the job is not in Cleveland."

"Let me see it."

Most honourable Sir: I humbly beg consideration for a position in your grand company . . .

"Who are you writing this to?"

"The president," said Miguel Mayor.

I am once a student of Dr. Ramiro Gutierrez of the Hydraulic Institute of Sevilla, Spain . . .

"Does the president know this Ramiro Gutierrez?"

"Oh, everybody is knowing him," Miguel Mayor assured, "he is the most famous expert in all Spain."

"Did he recommend this company to you?"

"No—I have said in my letter, if you look—"

An ancient student of Dr. Gutierrez, Salvador del Este, is actually a boiler expert who is being employed like supervisor is formerly a friend of mine . . .

"Is he still your friend?"

Whenever you say come to my city Miguel Mayor for talking I will be coming. I am working in Montreal since two years and am now wanting more money than I am getting here now . . .

"Well . . ." Dyer sighed.

"Sir—what I want from you is knowing in good English how to interview me by this man. The letters in Spanish are not the same to English ones, you know?"

I remain humbly at your orders . . .

"Why do you want to leave Montreal?"

"It's time for a change."

"Have you ever been to Cleveland?"

"I am one summer in California. Very beautiful there and hot like my country. Montreal is big port like Barcelona. Everybody mixed together and having no money. It is just a place to land, no?"

"Montreal? Don't be silly."

"I thought I come here and learn good English but where I work I get by in Spanish and French. It's hard, you know?" he smiled. Then he took a few steps back and gave his cuffs a gentle tug, exposing a set of jade cufflinks.

Dyer looked at the letter again and calculated how long he would be correcting it, then up at his student. How old is he? My age? Thirty? Is he married? Where do the Spanish live in Montreal? He looks so prosperous, so confident, like a male model off a page of *Playboy*. For an instant Dyer felt that his student was mocking him, somehow pitting his astounding confidence and wardrobe, sharp chin and matador's bearing against Dyer's command of English and mastery of the side streets, bistros, and ethnic restaurants. Mayor's letter was painful, yet he remained somehow competent. He would pass his interview, if he got one. What would he care about America, and the odiousness he'd soon be sup-

[13]

porting? It was as though a superstructure of exploitation had been revealed, and Dyer felt himself abused by the very people he wanted so much to help. It had to end someplace.

He scratched out the second "humbly" from the letter, then folded the sheet of foolscap. "Get it typed right away," he said. "Good luck."

"Thank you, sir," said his student, with a bow. Dyer watched the letter disappear in the inner pocket of the checkered sportscoat. Then the folding of the cashmere scarf, the draping of the camel's hair coat about the shoulders, the easing of the fur hat down to the rims of his ears. The meticulous filling of the pigskin gloves. Mayor's patent leather galoshes glistened.

"Good evening, sir," he said.

"*Buenas noches*," Dyer replied.

He hurried now, back down Sherbrooke Street to his daytime office where he could deposit his books. Montreal on a winter night was still mysterious, still magical. Snow blurred the arc lights. The wind was dying. Every second car was now a taxi, crowned with an orange crescent. Slushy curbs had hardened. The window of Holt-Renfrew's was still attractive. The legless dummies invited a final stare. He stood longer than he had earlier, in front of the sporty mannequin with a burgundy waistcoat, the mauve and blue ensemble, the jade cufflinks.

Good evening, sir, he could almost hear. The ascot, the shirt, the complete outfit, had leaped off the back of Miguel Mayor. He pictured how he must have entered the store with three hundred dollars and a prepared speech, and walked out again with everything off the torso's back.

I want that.

What, sir?

That.

The coat, sir?

Yes.

Very well, sir.

And *that.*

Which, sir?

All that.

"Absurd man!" Dyer whispered. There had been a moment of fear, as though the naked body would leap from the window, and legless, chase him down Sherbrooke Street. But the moment was passing. Dyer realized now that it was comic, even touching. Miguel Mayor had simply tried too hard, too fast, and it would be good for him to stay in Montreal until he deserved those clothes, that touching vanity and confidence. With one last look at the window, he turned sharply, before the clothes could speak again.

Eyes

You *jump into this business of a new* country cautiously. First you choose a place where English is spoken, with doctors and bus lines at hand, and a supermarket in a *centre d'achats* not too far away. You ease yourself into the city, approaching by car or bus down a single artery, aiming yourself along the boulevard that begins small and tree-lined in your suburb but broadens into the canyoned aorta of the city five miles beyond. And by that first winter when you know the routes and bridges, the standard congestions reported from the helicopter on your favorite radio station, you start to think of moving. What's the good of a place like this when two of your neighbors have come from Texas and the French paper you've dutifully subscribed to arrives by mail two days late? These French are all around you, behind the counters at the shopping center, in a house or two on your block; why isn't your little boy learning French at least? Where's the nearest *maternelle*? Four miles away.

In the spring you move. You find an apartment on a small side street where dogs outnumber children and the row houses resemble London's, divided equally between the rundown and remodeled. Your neighbors are the young personalities of French television who live on delivered chicken, or the old pensioners who shuffle down the summer sidewalks in pajamas and slippers in a state of endless recuperation. Your neighbors pay sixty a month for rent, or three hundred; you pay two-fifty for a two-bedroom flat where the walls have been replastered and new fixtures hung. The bugs *d'antan* remain, as well as the hulks of cars abandoned in the fire alley behind, where downtown drunks sleep in the summer night.

Then comes the night in early October when your child is coughing badly, and you sit with him in the darkened nursery, calm in the bubbling of a cold-steam vaporizer while your wife mends a dress in the room next door. And from the dark, silently, as you peer into the ill-lit fire alley, he comes. You cannot believe it at first, that a rheumy, pasty-faced Irishman in slate-gray jacket and rubber-soled shoes has come purposely to *your* small parking space, that he has been here before and he is not drunk (not now, at least, but you know him as a panhandler on the main boulevard a block away), that he brings with him a crate that he sets on end under your bedroom window and raises himself to your window ledge and hangs there nose-high at a pencil of light from the ill-fitting blinds. And there you are, straining with him from the uncurtained nursery, watching the man watching your wife, praying silently that she is sleeping under the blanket. The man is almost smiling, a leprechaun's face that sees what you cannot. You are about to lift the window and shout, but your wheezing child lies just under you; and what of your wife in the room next door? You could, perhaps, throw open the window and leap to the ground, tackle the man before he runs and smash his face into the bricks, beat him senseless then call the cops . . . Or better, find the camera, afix the flash, rap once at the window and shoot when he turns. Do nothing and let him suffer. *He is at your mercy,* no one will ever again be so helpless—but what can you do? You know, somehow, he'll escape. If you hurt him, he can hurt you worse, later, viciously. He's been a regular at your window, he's watched the two of you when you prided yourself on being young and alone and masters of the city. He knows your child and the park he plays in, your wife and where she shops. He's a native of the place, a man who knows the city and maybe a dozen such windows, who knows the fire escapes and alleys and roofs, knows the habits of the city's heedless young.

And briefly you remember yourself, an adolescent in another country slithering through the mosquito-ridden grassy fields behind a housing development, peering into those houses where newlyweds had not yet put up drapes, how you could spend five hours in a motionless crouch for a myopic glimpse of a slender arm reaching from the dark to douse a light. Then you hear what the man cannot; the creaking of your bed in the far bedroom, the steps of your wife on her way to the bathroom, and you see her as you never have before: blond and tall and rangily built, a north-Europe princess from a constitutional monarchy, sensuous mouth and prominent teeth, pale, tennis-ball breasts cupped in her hands as she stands in the bathroom's light.

"How's Kit?" she asks. "I'd give him a kiss except that there's no blind in there," and she dashes back to bed, nude, and the man bounces twice on the window ledge.

"You coming?"

You find yourself creeping from the nursery, turning left at the hall and then running to the kitchen telephone; you dial the police, then hang up. How will you prepare your wife, not for what is happening, but for what has already taken place?

"It's stuffy in here," you shout back, "I think I'll open the window a bit." You take your time, you stand before the blind blocking his view if he's still looking, then bravely you part the curtains. He is gone, the crate remains upright. "Do we have any masking tape?" you ask, lifting the window a crack.

And now you know the city a little better. A place where millions come each summer to take pictures and walk around must have its voyeurs too. And that place in all great cities where rich and poor co-exist is especially hard on the people in-between. It's health you've been seeking, not just beauty; a tough urban health that will save you money in the bargain, and when you hear of a place twice as large at half the rent, in a part of town free of Texans, English, and French, free of young actors and stewardesses who deposit their garbage in pizza boxes, you move again.

It is, for you, a city of Greeks. In the summer you move you attend a movie at the corner cinema. The posters advertise a war movie, in Greek, but the uniforms are unfamiliar. Both sides wear mustaches, both sides handle machine guns, both leave older women behind dressed in black. From the posters outside there is a promise of sex; blond women in slips, dark-eyed peasant girls. There will be rubble, executions against a wall. You can follow the story from the stills alone: mustached boy goes to war, embraces dark-eyed village girl. Black-draped mother and admiring young brother stand behind. Young soldier, mustache fuller, embraces blond prostitute on a tangled bed. Enter soldiers, boy hides under sheets. Final shot, back in village. Mother in black; dark-eyed village girl in black. Young brother marching to the front.

You go in, pay your ninety cents, pay a nickel in the lobby for a wedge of *halvah*-like sweets. You understand nothing, you resent their laughter and you even resent the picture they're running. Now you know the Greek for "Coming Attractions," for this is a gangster movie at least thirty years old. The eternal Mediterranean gangster movie set in Athens instead of Naples or Marseilles, with smaller cars and narrower roads, uglier women and more sinister killers. After an hour the movie flatters you. No one knows you're not a Greek, that you don't belong in this theater, or even this city. That, like the Greeks, you're hanging on.

Outside the theater the evening is warm and the wide sidewalks are clogged with Greeks who nod as you come out. Like the Ramblas in Barcelona, with children out past midnight and families walking back and forth for a long city block, the men filling the coffeehouses, the women left outside, chatting. Not a blond head on the sidewalk, not a blond head for miles. Greek music pours from the coffeehouses, flies stumble on the pastry, whole families munch their *torsades molles* as they walk. Dry goods are sold at midnight from the sidewalk, like New York fifty years ago. You're wandering happily, glad that you moved, you've rediscovered the innocence of starting over.

Then you come upon a scene directly from Spain. A slim blond girl in a floral top and white pleated skirt, tinted glasses, smoking, with bad skin, ignores a persistent young Greek in a shiny Salonika suit. "Whatsamatta?" he demands, slapping a ten-dollar bill on his open palm. And without looking back at him she drifts closer to the curb and a car makes a sudden squealing turn and lurches to a stop on the cross street. Three men are inside, the back door opens and not a word is exchanged as she steps inside. How? What refinement of gesture did we immigrants miss? You turn to the Greek boy in sympathy, you know just how he feels, but he's already heading across the street, shouting something to his friends outside a barbecue stand. You have a pocketful of bills and a Mediterranean soul, and money this evening means a woman, and blond means whore and you would spend it all on another blond with open pores; all this a block from your wife and tenement. And you hurry home.

Months later you know the place. You trust the Greeks in their stores, you fear their tempers at home. Eight bathrooms adjoin a central shaft, you hear the beatings of your son's friends, the thud of fist on bone after the slaps. Your child knows no French, but he plays cricket with Greeks and Jamaicans out in the alley behind Pascal's hardware. He brings home the oily tires from the Esso station, plays in the boxes behind the appliance store. You watch from a greasy back window, at last satisfied. None of his friends is like him, like you. He is becoming Greek, becoming Jamaican, becoming a part of this strange new land. His hair is nearly white; you can spot him a block away.

On Wednesdays the butcher quarters his meat. Calves arrive by refrigerator truck, still intact but for their split-open bellies and sawed-off hooves. The older of the three brothers skins the carcass with a small thin knife that seems all blade. A knife he could shave with. The hide rolls back in a continuous flap, the knife never pops the membrane over the fat.

Another brother serves. Like yours, his French is adequate. *"Twa lif d'hamburger,"* you request, still watching the operation on the rickety sawhorse. Who could resist? It's a Levantine treat, the calf's stumpy legs high in the air, the hide draped over the edge and now in the sawdust, growing longer by the second.

The store is filling. The ladies shop on Wednesday, especially the old widows in black overcoats and scarves, shoes and stockings. Yellow, mangled fingernails. Wednesdays attract them with boxes in the window, and they call to the butcher as they enter, the brother answers, and the women dip their fingers in the boxes. The radio is loud overhead, music from the Greek station.

"Une et soixante, m'sieur. Du bacon, jambon?"

And you think, taking a few lamb chops but not their saltless bacon, how pleased you are to manage so well. It is a Byzantine moment with blood and widows and sides of dripping beef, contentment in a snowy slum at five below.

The older brother, having finished the skinning, straightens, curses, and puts away the tiny knife. A brother comes forward to pull the hide away, a perfect beginning for a gameroom rug. Then, bending low at the rear of the glistening carcass, the legs spread high and stubby, the butcher digs in his hands, ripping hard where the scrotum is, and pulls on what seems to be a strand of rubber, until it snaps. He puts a single glistening prize in his mouth, pulls again and offers the other to his brother, and they suck.

The butcher is singing now, drying his lips and wiping his chin, and still he's chewing. The old black-draped widows with the parchment faces are also chewing. On leaving, you check the boxes in the window. Staring out are the heads of pigs and lambs, some with the eyes lifted out and a red socket exposed. A few are loose and the box is slowly dissolving from the blood, and the ice beneath.

The women have gathered around the body; little pieces are offered to them from the head and entrails. The pigs' heads are pink, perhaps they've been boiled, and hairless. The eyes are strangely blue. You remove your gloves and touch the skin, you brush against the grainy ear. How the eye attracts you! How you would like to lift one out, press its smoothness against your tongue, then crush it in your mouth. And you cannot. Already your finger is numb and the head, it seems, has shifted under you. And the eye, in panic, grows white as your finger approaches. You would take that last half inch but for the certainty, in this world you have made for yourself, that the eye would blink and your neighbors would turn upon you.

Words for the Winter

September, month of the winding down. For a month we've lived the charade of ruddy good health up in the mountains north of Montreal. Swimming, rowing, tramping up the mountain just behind our cabin, baking trout over the coals at night. Drinking from the last pure-water lake in the Laurentians, reading by sunlight on the dock, sleeping in the cool mountain air from dark till the sunrise at 5 A.M. This is how I dreamed it would be: water, trout, and mountains. And in this small way, I have succeeded.

Serge rows over around seven o'clock with two large trout, cleans them in our sink, and Erika spices them for baking. It was Serge who built our cabin and half the others on the lake after his family opened it up for exploitation. He's a Peugeot dealer in St-Jovite with a beard and a sordid past, and in the compulsive way of people who have painfully come through, he tells us about his failures, his vices, his present contentment. Like most reformed sinners and drinkers I've met, he is a mystic. "This lake, you know," he tells us in English, for emphasis, "he save my life. Every weekend now for ten year I am coming to him by myself. Without him, I am a dead man. Three time already, I am a dead man."

I have seen the scars. A knifing from his *voyou* days in Montreal. A cancerous lung. His heart. But he's a fit man now. He makes me feel that I'm only a teacher too young to have suffered and deserved the lake, but too old to ever learn the proper physical skills. To buy this cabin I simply answered a newspaper ad, got into his boat and saw those trout he'd caught that morning. As we talk, he cuts little wedges of pine to shore up our cabin and make the door fit tighter. He cuts cardboard to make the pump airtight. Unobtrusive skills I'll never master. Lurid stories I can only hope to copy, of gamblers in Acapulco, jail terms, a bankruptcy, an oath in an oxygen tent to be reborn.

The city lies an hour and a half to the south. We drop six hundred feet and gain two weeks of summer. A stagnant dome of dust and fumes squats over the city. September is still hot, street smells penetrate closed windows. It is a street of tenements, some of greystone, some of dark brick, some with porches, and some with the traditional winding outside staircases of old Montreal. The neighborhood has been French, then Jewish, then Italian, and now Greek, with Chinese and West Indians waiting their turn. A Ukrainian Church, a *ye-shiva*, an Esso station, and a Greek grocery store bracket the street. We rent a nine-room flat in a three-story tenement. The flat across the hall has been sub-divided; a large and violent family of Greeks in the back four rooms, two students and a Jamaican night watchman in the front three rooms, with one kept as a dining room, equipped with a stove and fridge. Above us a commune of hippies; above them, a nameless horde of student-age workers, French-Canadian, who often fight. In the single basement flat lives an extended family of Jamaicans with uncountable children all roughly the same age. Our four-year-old son plays with two of theirs; rugged, gentle boys of five and seven.

The winters are an agony. In January our broad summer street narrows to a one-lane rut, an icy *piste de luge* banked by walls of unmovable cars. I stand with the Greeks and West Indians at the bus stop, wrapped in double gloves, double socks, and a scarf under my stocking cap, stamping my feet under a fog of human warmth. We stand like cattle in a blizzard, edging closer than we would in summer, smoke and vapor rising through the wool, each of us dreaming of heat and coffee. The Greeks and West Indians must want to die.

You survive by subtraction. Pick a date: March 15, say. The coldest days bring wind and an arctic sun, much suffering, but one day less. Warmer days, those above zero, inevitably bring snow—and one day less. Some time in January we enter the trough, the two weeks of winter torpor when pipes burst and cars give out and the wind cuts viciously through the flat, rattling under the doors and around the windows—your tongue could stick to those icy windows—and water could boil on the ancient radiators. The sky is a pitiless, cloudless blue, and tons of sulphur are pushed into the shrunken air. The day is reached when the city voluntarily closes down. You cancel classes like everyone else, you eat whatever you find in the fridge, your child has a nosebleed every few minutes. It's then you think of your landlord in Florida, of your own days before coming here, when winter was short and bracing, a good time for steady work. Your students hobble to classes on their *après-ski* plaster casts—proud souvenirs of the climate they love. You think of the rings of winter that surround Montreal: caribou foraging north of the mountains, men in the mining camps, timber wolves riding the flat cars into the city, holing up in the cemeteries and living on suburban strays. We are in the dentist's chair for another forty days. Even Erika sleeps late, turns in early, and admits to constant headaches. Christopher suffers his nosebleeds and hasn't been out in twenty days. The mice have left us alone. The Jamaican children come up to play, riding tricycles through our endless flat.

Only the mailman still makes it through. By the time one of us dresses warmly enough to step out to the mail-slots, our letters have already been fished out of the mutilated slot—years of theft have left the brass doors buckled—and have been ripped into tiny pieces and dropped like an offering outside our door. Letters from Germany, computerized checks and bills, all the work of the Greek girl across the hall. She will go to stores for you. She will play with your boy when she finds him alone. And she will steal his toys and kick the smaller Jamaican girls when she finds them alone. Last summer her father beat her in the hall, in front of me and the Laflamme kids who live next door; a slim, scar-faced tyrant whose wife stood behind him, looking at her fingers. Laflamme's kids howled with pleasure, "Ooo,

Irène, va pleurer!" but she didn't, not for the moments that I could bear to watch. I wanted to protect her, for whatever she'd done, that bruised furtive little thing with the Anne Frank face. That cheat, that thief, that cunning wretched child.

I buy the traps six at a time and throw the whole thing out, when successful, in a single grand gesture, wasting a garbage sack but feeling cleaner. Laflamme's kids pick up all the sacks on garbage nights, and I've watched them, in their curiosity, untie the empty ones and dump out the mouse and trap, lift the spring and kick the mouse aside; thus saving a trap and garbage sack to take back home.

There are worse things than mice. The lake has taught us to live with black flies and leeches. Now the mice have lost their power to offend. Kit is fascinated, leaves peanuts for them in old jar lids. At night we hear the dragging of the lids, the busy tapping of tiny claws on the ancient linoleum. One got trapped with a peanut half-expelled. Their fur bloodless, eyes unclotted, they seem merely frozen in gesture. I'm almost afraid to lift that clamp from their neck, for fear if I did they'd rise to bite me, or slide unconscious up my sleeve.

This evening I was reading in the living room, the large front double room that looks out over the street. There came a tapping so low and rhythmic that I absorbed it into my reading. I hadn't wanted to leave the chair. But the tapping persisted and I knew it came from closer than I wanted to admit, from the parlor behind the sliding doors, where we keep the summer tires and suitcases. I could see the leather lid of Erika's suitcase panting from inside, as though it had an embolism. It was her old belted bag from Germany, the one she kept her secrets in, everything portable and priceless from her first twenty years. I could picture the inside of that bag as though I had X-ray vision, the mouse-nests of shredded paper. For a moment I allowed myself to think exactly what it meant about us, about me. I have stained her with the froth of mice, their birth and death, in all my dreams and failures.

I bent to touch the suitcase and a single mouse leaped out, squeezing between the lid and clasp where she'd forgotten to re-cinch the belts. A small black one. Without opening the lid, expecting to hear the chirping of a dozen more inside, I cradled the suitcase like a baby in my arms and carried it down the hall past Erika who was reading in the bedroom. I placed it flat in the dry bathtub. She followed me in, standing at the door.

"Did you kill it?"

"There may be more inside," I said.

The flat is long and cheap and full of pests. Four usable bedrooms and a dining room, a double living room, kitchen, and two studies. It costs us ninety dollars a month, plus heat. We took it at my insistence, after Erika decided to quit her job and return to school. I wanted to sink into the city, to challenge it like any other immigrant and go straight to its core. We painted everything when we moved, put down rugs and tried to grow plants. At night, by muted lamp, with our leather chairs, white tables, colorful paintings, the front room looks beautiful. But the rest of the flat has defeated us.

I return to the parlor. No squeals from the closet, but

I open it anyway, knocking the old shoes with a tube of Christmas wrapping paper, and the black little thing scurries out, under the door to the hall and down the hall past the bathroom, with me in pursuit. "Mouse in the hall," Erika calls out in an even voice, still on her knees and lifting papers out of the tub to give them a shake and a repacking. The mouse darts into the dining room, under the radiator where the linoleum has lifted and there must be a hole. I've spoken to Laflamme about it—he refused to act without the landlord's directive, and gave me a box of steel wool instead. "Stuff it under there," he said, "it's mouseproof." And the landlord stays in Florida until the first of April.

I can hear the mouse under the radiator. I can see the old lids they've dragged underneath.

"No mice," she announces from the bathroom. "But *do* something."

She snaps the locks, tightens the belts. I poke twice with the cardboard tube, but it's too thick to reach all the way.

"If there'd been mice in there I would have left you."

I'll have to force him out. The pipes are scalding hot.

"There are some things that would kill me," she says.

We have DDT in the back, an old Aerosol can for roaches, and I fetch it. She wouldn't leave, not literally. But she would retreat a little further, which is worse. Some things would kill me, too. There are old droppings on the pantry shelves where we store only hardware. Cold drafts along the wood—there's a hole somewhere, Monsieur Laflamme. *Il y a un trou dans la . . . dans le . . . pantry?* Moving here was going to perfect my

French, which remains what it always was: a nicely polished vintage car poking along a new expressway. A danger to myself and others. A tall can of Raid, cold to the touch, might do the trick. I lay down a cover of spray, until my eyes smart and the coughing begins.

"What are you spraying?" she calls.

"Guess."

"Is that you coughing—or it?"

Best not to speak. Better indeed to kill, with my shoe if necessary. First come the roaches, staggering up the walls and falling back. I hear activity under the coils, I see a shadow slinking along the molding, around the clumps of steel wool, in the shadow of the drapes and television. A slow shadow I prod once with the cardboard to knock into the open. He can barely walk, his front paws splay, his back legs drag. I douse him again from six inches out till his black coat glistens and he stops for good. His eyes are shining, his motion arrested, and he could kill a city of bugs by walking among them. I spray again, idly, and he doesn't move. I get a garbage sack and spread its top; then, the other tube of wrapping paper and chop-stick the mouse into the sack. There is a puddle of Raid beneath him, reflecting light like a lake of gasoline. If I had the man's Florida address, I'd send him this. I will move Erika's bag, then wash.

In the spring of this year, a tragedy. Nikos, a quiet boy of six who often played with the Jamaicans in our building, fell to his death from the second-floor balcony next door. I'd seen him sitting on the rail eating his lunch, and I'd waved. A second later he flashed silently across my vision, a white shirt striking the muddy yard with a whip-sharp crack. I was the only witness. I was afraid to touch him; his body heaved in agonies that seemed adult, one leg kicking in and out. I was screaming on the silent street, "Ambulance! Police! *Au secours!*" and the street slowly bristled to life. Women who never came out opened their doors and ran toward me, those squat Greek women with their hands flat on their cheeks as they ran, and I was still over the body screaming, "Did you call for help? Did you call the police?" but they fought to get to the boy. A single word was passed, *Nikos, Nikos,* and wailing began from the steps to the sidewalk as I pushed an older woman back. "Are you the mama? *Nikos's mama?*" but I didn't think she was and I pushed her till she fell. "Listen to me. Understand. His neck is broken. He cannot be touched—" But they were like the insane, their faces twisted around their open mouths and accusing eyes. *Oh, God, I had dreamed of loving the Greeks,* and now I wished to annihilate them. One of theirs lay injured and I stood accused—a man, a foreigner, tall and blond —and they attacked. From below my shoulders they leaped to hurl their spittle, to scratch my face, to rip my shirt and trenchcoat. I was consumed with hatred for them all, a desire to use my size and innocence, my strength and good intentions, to trample them, to will them back to Greece and their piggish lives in the dark. They pecked like a flock of avenging sparrows, and one finally broke through to throw herself on the child and roll his body over.

Her scream was the purest cry of agony and sorrow I have ever heard. In the distance, a siren. The women let me go; all they had wanted was to scream. I gained the sidewalk and started walking. I felt a pity for us all that I had never felt before. Next to me stood Irene, the mail thief from across the hall.

"Who was it that fell—Nickie?" she asked.

She kept up with me. I was almost running.

"He was a dumb kid anyway," she said.

"Try to think better of him now, Irene."

"He's my cousin. You should see the toys he's got up there. And he's a crybaby."

"He didn't cry this time, Irene, so cut it out."

"Those old women—wow, they really gave it to you, eh? I heard them talking and they thought you did it. They thought you're the devil or something—really crazy, eh?"

We were walking up the steps to our building, a father and daughter to anyone passing. "Irene—who's going to tell his mother?"

"I don't know. My ma is her sister. His pa went back to Greece a long time ago. That was pretty stupid of him playing up on the balcony like that, eh?"

For a moment, in my hatred, I thought she'd done it; shades of *The Bad Seed*, she'd been up there all along taking his toys and making his morning miserable. But no one had left the building. Accidents were still possible, even here. We were standing by the mailslots. Our letters, as usual, lay shredded on the steps.

"Irene—tell me one thing. Why do you tear up our mail?"

"Who says I do that? It was Nikos did it."

"Don't lie. I'm not going to hit you. I want to know *why*."

Her voice was a woman's; her face, Anne Frank's. "O.K. I'll tell you. But I won't say it again. Nikos said we should do it. I told him about the way you waited for the mail all the time. So he thought that would really get you mad. It was him that did it. See if it happens again."

"Listen: Nikos was an innocent little kid. You're the one that knows how to hurt. And you know I wouldn't go to your father because of what he'd do to you. You know I disapprove of that even more than stealing."

"Boy, you sure must think I know a lot," she said. "I don't even know what you're talking about." And with that she extracted a key from her purse and disappeared, singing softly, behind the outer door of her apartment.

Late April rain, the snow is down on the west-facing slopes. Our mail has been left alone. I am learning to appreciate small favors: mail, mouselessness, the stirrings of spring. I enter the apartment carrying two bags of groceries, and walk directly to the kitchen to begin unloading. I'd kicked the door shut, but left the key ring dangling outside. Then I went out again to fetch Kit from downstairs and drive down to McGill to pick up Erika from the library—and I discovered that the keys were gone. Stolen. No car keys, no way now of getting back inside. Even Laflamme was useless since we'd never trusted him with a spare key. I went downstairs and found Kit drawing on cardboard boxes that he and his friends had hauled in from the alley. The basement apartment is the worst I've seen, with a ceiling that drips, broken plaster, linoleum worn through to the mossy boards and children everywhere, holding sandwiches as they play. They have no furniture, only beds and a table to eat from. I ask the mother and the eldest daughter if I can leave him there while I take a bus to find my wife, to get a key.

"Daddy—I want to go with you," he calls, running to the door and dropping his peanut butter sandwich.

"You can't, dear. It's still cold and you don't have a coat."

"Get my coat."

"That is something I cannot do. You'll have to stay. Now let me go." He's clutching my trenchcoat, suddenly aware that I'm leaving him behind and not just letting him play.

"Kit—let go."

He gives a jerk just as I try to break free; I feel the seam of my trenchcoat opening up, tearing like a zipper as Kit and his friends giggle. "Goddammit!" I scream and before I know it I've freed my coat and seized him by the shoulders and begun to shake him violently. "I told you to let go, I told you twice. Why can't you listen! What do I have to do to make you listen?" His face is inches from mine and white with terror. In his eyes I can read his hope that I'm only playing, and I want to stamp that out too. "*Understand?*" I give him a final shake. Limp in my arms he belches, and part of his sandwich comes heaving out.

I run from the basement, from Kit's screaming, the twin halves of my trenchcoat flapping on my back like the pattern for an immensely fat man's pair of pants. *My keys, my keys.* Car, house, office and cabin. The locker in the basement, the trunks in the locker. The cabin is elaborately locked; I will have to smash a window. The car is locked, rolled up tight. Again a window. The front of my shirt is stained, the Greeks at the bus stop are staring at me.

At this moment, Irene must be in the flat. There is much to steal that we will never miss. Something infinitely small but infinitely complicated has happened to our lives, and I don't know how to present it—in its smallness, in its complication—without breaking down. I who live in dreams have suffered something real, and reality hurts like nothing in this world.

The Keeler

Stories

We do not rest satisfied with the present.
We anticipate the future as too slow in
coming, as if in order to hasten its course;
or we recall the past, to stop its too rapid
flight. So imprudent are we that we wander in
the times which are not ours, and do not
think of the only one which belongs to us;
and so idle are we that we dream of those
times which are no more, and thoughtlessly
overlook that which alone exists.

Blaise Pascal

Pensées

Extractions and Contractions

Student Power

Leaving my office on the twelfth floor and boarding the elevator with ten students, I have this winter's first seizure of claustrophobia. Eleven of us in heavy overcoats, crammed shoulder-to-shoulder in an overlit stainless steel box, burning up. The elevator opens on 11 and two students turn away, seeing that it's full. We stop on 10 but no one is waiting. We are trapped by the buttons other people press before they take the stairs. We will stop on every floor, it is one of those days, though we can take no one in and all of us, obviously, are dressed for the street. On 8 as the doors open and no one presses "C" to close them quickly, I have a sense of how we must appear to any onlooker— like a squad of Gothic statuary, eyes averted upward, silent, prayerful. On 7 I sense there will be a student waiting as the door opens. He looks in, smiles, and we smile back. The doors do not close and we wait. He opens his briefcase and assembles a machine gun. We cannot move; we are somehow humiliated by overcrowding. No one presses "C." A burst of fire catches us all, economically gunned down by a grinning student. The doors close and do not open again until we tumble out in the main lobby.

The Street

Early November is colder this year than last. Twelve floors up, without windows, I forget about the cold. I have been reading Faulkner for five hours and haven't thought once of winter. I have been thinking, in fact, that with my citizenship papers I can now apply for government support in the summer. I could have before, but it didn't seem right.

It is cruel to confront the streets now: snowless but windy and in the lower 20s. Such mildness will not return until late March. November and March, deadly months. Depressing to think the dentist, like winter, is waiting. The cold wind on a bad tooth anticipates so much. I try to remember these streets as they were in June; a sidewalk cafe, the devastating girls in the briefest skirts and bra-less sweaters. These streets had so many tourists in the summer, forever asking directions and making me feel at home. At the end of the block parked in a taxi space, I spot a modest car with snow on the trunk and Maryland plates. On the left edge of the back bumper is a tattered *McCarthy for President* sticker and on the right, as I kick off a little snow, is the red-framed bilingual testament: *I'm Proud to Be a Canadian/Je suis fier d'être canadien.*

The Dentist

My teeth, my body, my child, my wife and the baby she is carrying are all in the hands of immigrants. All Jews. I do not know how this develops; because I am an immigrant too, perhaps. Our friends warned us against the indigenous dentists. Between hockey pucks and Pepsi caps, they said, Quebec teeth are only replaced, never filled.

This dentist's office is in a large, formerly brick office building that was stripped to its girders over the summer and then refaced with concrete panels and oblong windows. Inside, however, not a change. The corridors are still reminiscent of older high schools, missing only the rows of olive drab lockers. The doors are still darkly varnished and gummy from handling. The doctors and accountants still have their names in black on stippled glass. All this, according to Dr. Abramovitch, pains a dentist, whose restorative work is from the inside out. "Rotten inside," he snorts, poking my tooth but meaning the building. He is a man of inner peace, rumored to be a socialist. The rest of our doctors are socialists. His degrees are in Hebrew but for one that puzzles me more, in Latin. I am in the chair waiting for the freeze to take effect before I realize that *Monte Regis* means Montreal. I then remember a novel I have just read, a French-Canadian one, in which the narrator, a vendor of hot dogs, must decide on a name for his hot dog stand. The purists suggest *Au roi du chien chaud*. He chooses *Au roi du hot dog*. The author, I am told, is a separatist. I wonder if he cares that at least one outsider has read him. Poor Montreal, I now think, puts up with so much.

There is a battle this afternoon to save a tooth. The pulp is lost but the enamel is good. It is cheaper, he explains, to pull the tooth. But after pulling there must be a bridge and years later, another one. But pulling only the nerve (his brow smooths out) and packing the canal, though the work is tedious and expensive, is lavishly recommended. "I get forty-five for a nerve job, ten for a straight extraction," he says. *Pulling a nerve* is a sinister phrase, smacking of an advanced, experimental technique. But he is appealing, I can see, to all that is aesthetic in dentistry. No McTeague, this man, though his wrists bulge with competence. His extractions have been praised. I debate denying him any nerve, for with a numb jaw I can play the hero. *Lace the boot tighter, Doc. I gotta lead my men* . . . Finally, though, no John Wayne stuff for me. I consent, and he rams a platinum wire up the holes he has drilled, plunges it up and down then pulls it out, yellow with nerve scum. This is not how I pictured my nerve, though I had never hoped to look at a nerve, surely not my own, surely not this afternoon when I left my office. Brain surgery, too, I am told, is painless after cutting through the skull. I can hear the platinum probe grinding in my cheekbone nearly under my eye and I think of those pharmaceutical ads that used to appear in the *National*

Geographic of Incas performing brain surgery, spitting cocaine juice into the open skull as they cut.

"Success," he pronounces. He is happy, the tooth will drain, in a week he'll pack it. Leaving, I have my doubts. No John Wayne, certainly, I'm beginning to feel like Norman Mailer. A nerve ripped from my body at thirty. I am a young man, haven't deteriorated much since twenty-one, expect to remain the same at least till thirty-five. But somehow, some day, some *minute*, the next long decline begins to set in. At forty I will be middle-aged. At forty-five, twenty-five years from my grave. When does it start—with a chipped tooth? A broken nose? A broken leg even? Oh, no. It begins in choices. The road downhill is slick with fat and fallen hair and little pills. Bad styles and bad convictions. Pain killers, contraceptives, tranquilizers, and weak erections. Pulled nerves.

St. Catherine Street

From the dentist's, east on St. Catherine is an urban paradise. No finer street exists in my experience, even in November. St. Catherine should be filmed without dialogue or actors, just by letting the crowds swarm around a mounted camera and allowing a random sound track to pick up the talk, doppler-ing in and fading out, from every language in the world.

But west on St. Catherine, especially in November, is something else. Blocks of low buildings after Guy Street, loan offices on top and business failures down below. Auto salesrooms forever changing franchises, drugstores offering two-hour pregnancy tests, news and tobacco stands, basement restaurants changing nationalities. But if it can be afforded, or if one lives only with a wife, a convenient location. Someday Montreal will have its Greenwich Village and these short streets between St. Catherine and Dorchester will be the center.

I stop at an unlighted tobacconist's for the papers. One window bin is full of pipes and tins of tobacco, the other of dusty sex magazines from every corner of the Western World. The owner stands all day at the door and opens it only if you show an interest. Otherwise, it's locked, without lights. I stop in daily for my *Star* and *Devoir*. I always have two dimes because he keeps no observable change. He always responds, "*Merci.*" His face implies that he has suffered; also that he survives now in his darkened store by selling far more than the *Star*, *La Presse*, and all the Greek and German stag magazines. I have seen men enter the store and say things I couldn't understand and the owner present them with Hungarian, with Yiddish, with Ukrainian, with Latvian papers. Then they chat. Perhaps he speaks no English and just a word or two of French. Like my dentist, a man, ultimately, of mystery.

My Wife

Is it most significant that I say first she is a Ph.D. teaching at McGill and making more than I; or that she is the mother of our 5-year-old boy, and is now eight months pregnant and still teaching? Or that she is Indian and is one of those small radiant women one sees on larger campuses, their red or purple *sari*-ends billowing under Western overcoats? I'm home early to let the frozen jaw thaw and to see if the nerveless tooth will keep me from lecturing tonight. My wife should be in her office and our son at the sitter's.

The apartment seems emptier than usual; there's been some attempt at tidying, the lights are off and the afternoon gloom through the Fiberglas curtains is doubly desolate. I drop the briefcase, turn on the lights in the front room, then put coffee water on to boil in the dark narrow kitchen. Roaches scurry as I hit the light. I realize, on touching the cups, that the heat is low— maybe off. We have only five rooms but a very long hall; it curves twice and divides the apartment sharply. It costs us a great deal.

There is nothing distinctive about our place: given our double incomes, our alleged good taste, our backgrounds, this becomes distinctive. Other Indian, or semi-Indian, couples we know keep a virtual bazaar of silks and brasses and hempen rugs and eat off the floor at least once a week. Burn fresh incense every day. And though I do not like them, I sometimes envy them. There are days in November even without aching teeth that I realize how little I've done to improve our lives, how thwarted my sense of style has become.

I am sipping coffee when I hear the toilet flush in the rear of the apartment. I hurry back and find my wife rearranging the covers over her belly. She smiles and tells me to sit and keep time while she rests.

Contractions

Starting three hours earlier she's been having regular contractions of a mild variety; so mild that she hasn't bothered to call me. The cycle is steady but speeding up. "I'm sorry I haven't done the shopping," she says, smiling like a Hemingway heroine whose pain would crush a man. She assures me the contractions are light—almost delicious. Indians like massages, have special names for pressures and positions; it is something I have learned, something I can administer. "It's a false alarm," she insists. Nevertheless I decide to call Dr. Lapp. He seems ignorant of the case until I remind him that my wife is the Indian lady. "Ah, yes," he says, "don't panic." I am to take her in only if they get severe and come every two minutes.

"This is silly," she protests when they begin coming every two minutes. "I'm actually looking forward to them." She wants me to leave her at home and go back to school to eat and prepare my lecture. But I stand by my duty: pack her bag, call the sitters and tell them I'll pick up our boy around 10:30. They offer to have him spend the night, but I refuse. I want him with me.

The Hospital

We live just off St. Catherine, just where we want to be, but the hospital is suburban, in the deadly western sections, because all of Dr. Lapp's patients live there. We do not have a French doctor because, I suppose, of the rumored Catholic position on the primacy of the fetus. Dr. Lapp is from Boston but interned at McGill and for some reason, stayed. One doesn't trust a people until he trusts their doctors. This suburban hospital is reached by a three-dollar taxi ride. It fits into the neighborhood like a new church or modern school: low, long, red-brick, like every duplex on every street in the far western sections of Montreal. This is where my colleagues live; this is all they know of Montreal if, like me, they came here late: a bus line, a transfer point, the Metro stops, and school. Some shopping, some bookstore browsing, a downtown bank, a movie or two a month. None of them speaks a dozen words of French.

The doors of this hospital are marked: TIREZ/PULL, POUSSEZ/PUSH, and beyond the CAISSE/RECEPTIONIST, I see a sign: ASCENSEUR/ELEVATOR. For some reason I am thinking of a little test I once administered to some friends of mine in the English Department, and not of my wife, who is being admitted. It was a recognition test. All of the men had either been born or had lived at least five years in Montreal. I supplied some everyday words and asked if they could give equivalents in English, and some of the words, I recall, were *tirez, poussez,* and *défense de stationner*, and *arrêtez*. A man who owned a car identified both *arrêtez* and *sortie*. The others felt embarrassed and a little defensive. They told me that I should give such a test to some of the others, those who were harder to know and not quite so friendly, who lived in converted stables and in lofts down in the old city, whose second wives were French-Canadian and whose children went to rugged little *lycées* in Outremont. Those men were, admittedly, a little frightening. Also a little foolish. Is there nothing in-between? I wonder now what I was trying to prove my first year here with my evening courses in conversational French, my subscriptions to French magazines, my pride in reserving English for school and home, no place else. The depth of my commitment—to trivia.

Mongolism

Secretly I have been worrying that this second child will be Mongoloid. It seems that the papers and all the polite journals that flood our house have recently featured technical articles for the common reader on Mongolism. I know the statistics and I know what to look for even in a newborn infant. Position of the ears, size of tongue, bridge of nose, shape of feet, length of fingers. Blood, heart, lungs. The options: to commit him on sight to a home that will clean him, feed him, and let him die from the simplest illness; or to take him home and try to make him comfortable, all the time hoping that his weakened organs will overcome our love, our guilt, and fail him. Strangely, I do not fear anything physical. Because I am a professor and tend to minimize the physical? Because I seek punishment for the way we live, what we're doing to our boy who deserves better, with too many sitters and too much unlicensed television while we read and prepare? I support, in a bloodless and abstract way, euthanasia. Youth in Asia. I fear for the child because I refuse to doubt myself? I fear for the child because I fear even more my intentions toward him?

I remember the night he must have been conceived. My wife had been off her pills, for they make her sick too many mornings. She would vomit and teach, vomit and teach. I was sick with migraine. We had been quiet in bed. I gave her a kiss and turned away. A few minutes later, as I turned back in the dark, my lips brushed her nose. She had turned toward me, not away, and suddenly it was like discovering a beautiful stranger in my bed; there was nothing tender that night, nothing to become this child like his begetting. The only good sign. As for the rest, no health can come from something so unplanned, from parents so slovenly, an apartment so pest-infested and uninviting.

Evening Lecture

Another three-dollar ride home, quick change from possible paternity clothes, no supper or preparations, heat definitely gone, then a brisk walk down St. Catherine to school. Even in winter, when the weather can be the most unpleasant on the continent, I've found myself surfacing from the Metro and gawking at the buildings and people rather than moving on, out of the cold. Tonight, maybe a father for the second time, I walk slowly, smiling. I'll never be quite at home here, though now even a citizen; I'm as much a stranger in my way as the others that I know. Colleagues in the suburbs, legendary swingers down in the stables near the docks—this city makes fools of us all.

Then I think that living here is perhaps a low-grade art experience. I feel the life of the sidewalk, feel content for inexplicable reasons, simply for being here. Where else in the world is *Englais* spoken? I read in the paper of a French-Canadian student leader explaining in English why he demonstrated: *We are not complotting,* he said. *We are manifesting for more subventions.* And I understood every word. I shouldn't complain of those western suburbs and of the isolation of the housewives that I teach, nor should I worry about my tolerant, scholarly friends who see so little around them. Perhaps they see beyond the obvious, beyond the neutralizing bilingualism that surrounds them. Perhaps I'm only stuck on the obvious.

There are hundreds, thousands of evening students milling along the boulevard and side streets in front of the school. The boulevard is five lanes wide but pinched to a trickle while parents, boy friends, and taxis drop off students. I am caught in a crowd moving slowly toward the revolving doors, and I am thinking now only of the lecture, wondering how I'll pick up my boy after the lecture and get him fed and dressed for school in the morning and finally—Lord—what we'll do if this is the real baby, tonight, six weeks before the Christmas holidays when he was providentially due. Must everything we do be so tightly budgeted? In *Buddenbrooks* the hero dies prematurely after a dental visit, without a nerve even being discussed. I could die tonight of a dozen things, all deserved.

An Indian

From the hundreds in front of the school, I am grabbed by an Indian man in a high Tashkent fur cap and lamb's-wool coat. He seizes an elbow as though in anger, his gloved fingers press painfully through my coat and sports jacket.

"This is not the Krishna Temple?"

I give him directions.

He frowns, presses me harder, for this does not please him. Crowds of students swirl around us. Why seize me, I want to cry, the scent of a martyred wife is that strong? He can tell? But his grip is serene, impersonal, and painful.

"Nevertheless, I will enter," he says, "this place."

"Fine."

"I must present documents." Again, he is asking. I tell him he mustn't.

"What this place is?"

"A university." I know this will confuse him. This is the largest academic building in the Commonwealth, I am told, but it looks nothing like a school. He presses harder.

"It is very late."

The lobby is packed like a department store, which it already resembles with its escalators and high ceilings. We push through a door, two-by-two, and his grip loosens until I begin to pull away.

"You are not a student," he says, or asks, "you are," and he strains as though making a difficult judgment, "another thing."

And then suddenly he drops my arm and takes off through the crowd. No chance to catch him, *shake him*, and demand how he found me, of all people, tonight of all nights. A brown angel, not of death but perhaps of impairment? My wife in pain? Dying? The baby? Me? I push to the escalator then turn quickly in order to find him in the lobby and it is not difficult; he cuts through the crowd as though somehow charmed, just as I had feared. Students part to let him pass, even those who do not see him.

I call my wife during the intermission. The contractions have stopped, she's had a pill and will spend the night. Home after breakfast. A little fatigued, they said. She is preparing her Wednesday lecture.

The Night

From school I take a taxi to the baby-sitter's—two dollars—and gather my son in his blanket and carry him back to the waiting cab. Another two-fifty. I get home

to find it much colder, the first heat failure of the winter.
What does this mean? I put him in our bed, look for
extra blankets but can't find them, call the landlord's
answering service, then crawl in with my boy, fully
dressed in the clothes I lectured in.

Sometime deep and cold in the night he pulls the
cover from me and tugs my hand until I waken. He is
crying, standing on the rug with his pajama bottoms
down and pointing toward the bathroom. I follow his
hand and see—in several peaks—the movement he'd run
to the bathroom to prevent. The largest mounds are on
the rug; several more, including what he's stepped on
and carried far down the hall and all over the bathroom
floor, is on the hardwood overlap around the rug.

It is three in the morning. The time of the crack-up.
I stoop, shivering, over piles of gelatinous shit on our
only decent possession, an Irish wool rug. My boy, guilty
and frightened, steps up his crying. *Back to bed*, I snap,
weary but forgiving, and he counters, "Where's
Mommy?" but there is no time to explain. "You're
bad!" he cries, and hits me, screams louder, and I'm
close to tears. Can I just leave it, I wonder, not so much
wanting to but not knowing where to start. Then I carry
him to the bathroom, clean his feet, his bottom, and
return him to bed. I have never been so awake; I can see
perfectly with no lights on. I mop the hall and bathroom floor. In the half-dark kitchen I grab a knife and
cereal bowl, then the rug shampoo and brush from an
undisturbed plastic tub under the sink. I scrape the rug
with the knife, try to pick up everything I can see with

the help of the bathroom light, then dip the brush in hot soapy water and begin to scrub.

For a minute or two it goes well, then I notice glistening shapes staggering from the milky foam; the harder I press, the more appear. *My child has roaches*, his belly is teeming, full of bugs, a plague of long brown roaches is living inside him, thriving on our neglect. The roaches creep and dart in every direction, I whack them with the wooden brush but more are boiling from the foam and now they appear on my hand and arm. I see two on the shoulder of my white shirt. I shout but my throat is closed after an evening lecture—I sputter phlegm. These are not my son's; they are the rug's. The other side of this fine Irish rug that we bought for a house in the suburbs that we later decided against, this rug that we haven't turned in months and haven't sent out to be cleaned, is a sea of roaches. I drop the brush and look underneath. Hairpins and tufts of tissue: an angry wave of roaches walking the top of the brush and glistening in the fibers like wet leaves beginning to stir. *My brush*, I want to cry: the brush was my friend. I pick it up and run with it down the hall, the filthiest thing I've ever held. I hear the roaches dropping to safety on the floor. It occurs to me as I open the apartment door and then the double doors of the foyer, and as I fling the brush over one curb of parked cars, that a drop of soapy water anywhere in this apartment would anger the roaches: the drawers, the mattresses, the good china, the silverware at night. First brushes, then rugs, and anything fine we might possibly buy or try to preserve; everything will yield to roaches. All those golden children of our joint income, infested.

Morning Dawns

After the rug I do the floors again, even the kitchen and hall and living room. I rewash every dish, spray ammonia where I can't reach. Then I throw away the mops and sponges, as the pharaohs killed their slaves, then killed the slaves that had dug the graves, killed the slaves that killed the slaves . . . not a sponge, a rag, a bucket, a mop, a scrap of newspaper or length of paper-toweling left. At six o'clock in a freezing apartment, with an aching former nerve, I open the windows and clean the outside, wiping with my handkerchief, then throwing it away. By six o'clock near-light, by street and alley lamp, the place looks clean and ready for people. Ready for more than our basic used Danish. *Ready for youth*, I let myself think: for sitars in the corner, fishnets on the wall, posters, teakwood chests. In with pillows and garish cottons, out with sofas, tables, and doors. Sitting on the Danish sofa, wrapped in my overcoat, I can almost hear the guests arriving, smell the incense, sway to Ravi Shankar records . . .

But I'm not young, anymore.

I part the Fiberglas curtains. It is snowing heavily now, with tiny flakes. The cars will be stuck—thank God we walk. The brush I threw is white, straddled by the tracks of an early car. After such roaches, what improvement? A loft, a farmhouse, a duplex five miles out? Five years in this very place living for the city, the city our prize. For what we've caught, stopped, saved, we could have camped along St. Catherine Street. Holding onto nothing, because we were young and didn't need it. Always thinking: no compromise. Always thinking: there is nowhere else we'd rather be. Nowhere else we can be, now. Old passports, pulled nerves, resting in offices. I think of my friends, the records they cry over, silly poems set to music, and I could cry as well. For them, for us. At the window I watch the men brush off their windshields, hear the engines trying to start. My son will soon be waking. I drop the curtains and go to put on water.

Going to India

1

A *month before we left I read a horror* story in the papers. A boy had stepped on a raft, the raft had drifted into the river. The river was the Niagara. Screaming, with rescuers not daring to follow, pursued only by an amateur photographer on shore, he was carried over the Falls.

It isn't death, I thought, it's watching it arrive, this terrible omniscience that makes it not just death, but an execution. The next day, as they must, they carried the photos. Six panels of a boy waving ashore, the waters eddying, then boiling, around his raft. The boy wore a T-shirt and cut-off khakis. He fell off several feet before the Falls. Who would leave a raft, what kind of madman builds a raft in Niagara country? Children in Niagara country must have nightmares of the Falls, must feel the earth rumbling beneath them, their pillows turning to water.

I was raised in Florida. Tidal waves frightened me as a child. So did "Silver Springs," those underground rivers that converge to feed it. Blind white catfish. I could hear them as a child, giant turtles snorting and grinding under my pillow.

My son is three years old, almost four. He will be four in India. Born in Indiana, raised in Montreal—what possible fears could he have? He finds the paper, the six pictures of the boy on a raft. He inspects the pictures and I grieve for him. I am death-driven. I feel compassion, grief, regret, only in the face of death. I was slow, fat and asthmatic, prone to sunburn, hookworms, and chronic nosebleeds. My son is lean and handsome, a tennis star of the future, and I've tried to keep things from him.

"What is that boy doing, Daddy?"

"I think he's riding a raft."

"But how come he's waving like that?"

"He's frightened, I think."

"Look—he felled off it, Daddy."

"I know, darling."

"And there's a water hill there, Daddy. Everything went over the hill."

"Yes, dear. The boy went over the water hill."

"And now he knows one thing, doesn't he, Daddy?"

"What does he know?"

"Now he knows what being dead is like."

2

A month from now we'll be in India. I've begun to feel it, I've been floating for a week now, afraid to start anything new. Friends say to me, "You still here?" not just in disappointment, more in amazement. They've already discarded the Old Me. "Weren't you going to India? What happened—chicken out?" They expect transmutation. "I *said* June," I tell them, but they'd heard April. "I'd be afraid to go," one friend, an artist, tells me. "There are some things a man can't take. Some changes are too great." I tell him I *am* afraid, but that I have to go.

I never cared for India. My only interest in the woman I married was sexual; that she was Indian did not excite me, nor was I frightened. Convent-trained, Brahmanical, well-to-do, Orthodox and Westernized at once, Calcutta-born, speaker of eight languages, she had simply overwhelmed me. We met in graduate school at Indiana. Both of us were in Comparative Literature, and she was returning to Calcutta to marry a forty-year-old research chemist selected by her father. Will you marry him? I asked. Yes, she said. Will you be happy? Who can say, she said. Probably not. Can you refuse? I asked. It would be bad for my father, she said. Will you marry me? I asked, and she said, "Yes, of course."

It was Europe that drove me mad.

Five years ago I threw myself at Europe. For two summers I did things I'll never do again, living without money enough for trolley fare, wakening beside new women, wondering where I'd be spending the next night, with whom, how I'd get there, who would take me, and finally not caring. Coming close, those short Swedish nights those fetid Roman nights, those long Paris nights when the *auberge* closed before I got back and I would walk through the rain dodging the Arabs and queers and drunken soldiers who would take me for an Arab, coming close to saying that life was passionate and palpable and worth the pain and effort and whoever I was and whatever I was destined to be didn't matter. Only living for the moment mattered and even the hunger and the insults and the occasional jab in the kidneys didn't matter. It all reminded me that I was young and alive, a hitchhiker over borders, heedless of languages, speaking just enough of everything to cover my needs, and feeling responsible to no one but myself for any jam I got into.

I would have given anything to stay and I planned my life so that I could come back.

Not once did I think of India. Missionary ladies from Wichita, Kansas, went to India. Retired buyers for Montgomery Ward took around-the-world flights and got heart attacks in Delhi bazaars. I was only interested in Europe.

At graduate school in Indiana I was doing well, a Fulbright was in the works, my languages were improving, and a lifetime in Europe was drawing closer. Then I met the most lushly sexual woman I had ever seen. Reserved and intelligent, she confirmed in all ways my belief that perfection could not be found in anything American.

But even then India failed to interest me. I married Anjali Chatterjee, not a culture, not a subcontinent.

3

When we married, the Indian community of Indiana disowned her. Indian girls were considered too innocent to meet or marry Western boys although hip Indian boys always married American girls. Anjali was dropped from the Indian Society, and only one Indian, a Christian dietician from Goa, attended our wedding. So the break was clean, my obligations minimal. I had her to myself.

Her parents were hesitant, but cordial. Also helpless. They had my horoscope cast after the marriage, but never told us the result. They asked about my family, and we lied. To say the least, I come from uncertain stock. My parents had been twice-divorced before divorcing each other. Four of the five languages I speak are rooted in my family, each grandparent speaking something different, and the fifth, Russian, reflects a secret sympathy that would destroy her parents if they knew. I have scores of half brothers and sisters, cousins-in-law, aunts and uncles known by the cars they drive, or by the rackets they operate. My family is broad and fluid and, though corrupt, fabulously unsuccessful. Like gypsies they cover the continent, elevating a son or two into Law (a sensible precaution), some into the civil service, others into the Army and only one into the university. My instructions for this trip are simple: do not mention divorce. My parents are retired, somewhat infirm, and comfortably off. After a while we can let one die (when we need the sympathy), and a few months later the second can die of grief. They will leave their fortune to charity.

4

E. M. Forster, you ruined everything. Why must every visitor to India, every well-read tourist, expect a sudden transformation? I, too, feel that if nothing amazing happens, the trip will be a waste. I've done nothing these past two months. I'm afraid to start anything new in case I'll be a different person when I return. And what if this lassitude continues? Two fallow months before the flight, three months of visiting, then what? What the hell is India like anyway?

I remember my Florida childhood and the trips to Nassau and Havana, the bugs and heat and the quiver of joy in a simple cold Coco-Cola, and the pastel, rusted, rotting concrete, the stench of purple muck too rank to grow a thing, to ever be charmed by the posters of palms and white sand beaches. Jellyfish, sting rays, sand sharks, and tidal waves. Roaches as long as my finger, scorpions in my shoe, worms in my feet. Still, it wasn't India. Country of my wife, heredity of my son.

Will *his* children speak of their lone white grandfather as they settle back to brown-ness, or will it be their legendary Hindu grandmother, as staggering to them as Pushkin's grandfather must have been to him? Appalling, that I, a comparatist who needs five languages, should be mute and illiterate in my wife's own tongue!

And worse, not to care, not for Bengali or Hindi or even Sanskrit.

I thought you were going to India—

I am, I am.

But—

Next week. Next week.

And don't forget those pills, man. Take those little pills.

5

We are going by charter, which still sets us back two thousand dollars. Two thousand dollars just on kerosene! Another two thousand for a three-month stay; hundreds more in preparation, in drip-dry shirts, in bras and lipsticks for the flocks of cousins; bottles of aftershave and Samsonite briefcases for their husbands. A complete set of the novels of William Faulkner for a cousin writing her dissertation. Oh, weird, weird, what kind of country am I visiting? To prepare myself I read. *Nothing could prepare me for Calcutta*, writes a welltraveled Indian on his return. City of squalor, city of dreadful night, of riots and stabbings, bombings added to pestilence and corruption. Somewhere in Calcutta, squatting or dying, two aged grandmothers are waiting to see my wife, to meet her *mlechha* husband, to peer and poke at her outcaste child. In Calcutta I can meet my death quite by accident, swept into a corridor of history for which I have no feeling. I can believe that for being white and American and somewhat pudgy I deserve to die—somewhere, at least—but not in Calcutta. Receptacle of the world's grief, Calcutta. *Indians, even the richest, are corrupted by poverty;* Americans, even the poorest (I add), are corrupted by wealth. How will I react to beggars? To servants? Worse: how will my wife?

6

I know from experience that when Anjali dabs the red *teep* on her forehead, when the gold earrings are brought out, when the miniskirts are put away and the gold necklace and bracelets are fastened to her neck and arms (how beautiful, how inevitable, gold against Indian skin), when the good silk saris with the golden threads are unfolded from the suitcases, that I have lost my wife to India. Usually it's just for an evening, in the homes of McGill colleagues in Hydraulics or Genetics, or visitors to our home from Calcutta, who stay with us for a night or two. And I fade away those evenings, along with English and other familiar references. Nothing to tell me that the beautiful woman in the pink sari is my wife except the odd wink during the evening, a gratuitous reference to my few accomplishments. The familiar mixture of shame and gratitude; that she was born and nurtured for someone better than I, richer, at least, who would wrap her in servants, a house of her own, a life of privilege that only an impoverished country can provide. One evening I can take. But three months?

7

Our plane will leave from New York. We go down two days early to visit our friends, the Gangulis. To spend some money, buy the last-minute gifts, another suitcase, enjoy the air-conditioning, and eat our last rare steaks. I've just turned twenty-seven; at that age, one can say of one's friends that none are accidental, they all fulfill a need. In New York three circles of friends almost coincide; the writers I know, the friends I've taught with or gone to various schools with, and the third, the special ones, the Indo-Americans, the American girls and their Indian husbands.

Deepak is an architect; Susan was a nurse. Deepak, years before in India, was matched to marry my wife. She was still in Calcutta, he was at Yale, and he approved of her picture sent by his father. One formality remained—the matching of their horoscopes. And they clashed. Marriage would invite disaster, deformed children most likely. He didn't meet her until his next trip to India when he'd gone to look over some new selections. Alas, none were beautiful enough and he returned to New York to marry the American girl he'd been living with all along.

Deepak's life is ruled by his profound good taste, his perfect, daring taste. Like a prodigy in chess or music he is disciplined by a Platonic conception of a yet-higher order, one that he alone can bring into existence. Their apartment in the East Seventies was once used as a movie set. It is subtly Indian, yet nothing specifically Indian strikes the eye. One must sit a moment, sipping a gin, before the underlying Eastern-ness erupts from the steel and glass and leather. The rug is Kashmiri, the tables teak, the walls are hung with Saurashtrian tapestries—what's so Western about it? The lamps are stone-based, chromium-necked, arching halfway across the room, the chairs are stainless steel and white leather, adorned with Indian pillows. It is a room in perfect balance, like Deepak; like his marriage, perhaps. So unlike ours, so unlike us. Our apartment in Montreal is furnished in Universal Academic, with Danish sofas and farm antiques, everything sacrificed to hold more books. The Who's-Afraid-of-Virginia-Woolf style.

But he didn't marry Anjali. I did. He married Susan, and Susan, though uncomplaining and competent, is also plain and somewhat stupid. Very pale, a near-natural blonde, but prone to varicosed chubbiness. An Indian's dream of the American girl. And so lacking in Deepak's exquisite taste that I can walk into their place and in thirty seconds *feel* where she had been sitting, where she'd walked from, everything she'd rearranged or brushed against. Where she's messed up the Platonic harmony even while keeping it clean. Still, Deepak doesn't mind. He cooks the fancy meals, does the gourmet shopping: knows where to find mangoes in the dead of winter, where the firmest cauliflower, the freshest *al dente* shrimp, the rarest spices, are sold. When Deepak shops he returns with twenty small packages individually wrapped and nothing frozen. When Susan returns it's with an A & P bag, wet at the bottom.

When the four of us are dining out, the spectators (for we are always on view) try to rearrange us: Deepak and Anjali, Susan and me. Deepak is tall for a Bengali—six-two perhaps—and impressively bearded now that it's the style. He could be an actor. A friend once described him as the perfect extra for a Monte Carlo scene, the Indian prince throwing away his millions, missing only a turban with a jewel in the center.

How could he and Anjali have a deformed child?

I'm being unfair. He is rich and generous, and there is another Deepak behind the man of perfect taste. He told me once when our wives were out shopping, that he'd tried to commit suicide, back in India. The Central Bank had refused him foreign exchange, even after he'd been accepted at Yale. He'd had to wait a year while an uncle arranged the necessary bribes, spending the time working on the uncle's tea estate in Assam. The uncle tried to keep him on a second year, claiming he had to wait until a certain bureaucrat retired; Deepak threw himself into a river. A villager lost his life in saving him, the uncle relented, a larger bribe was successful and Deepak the architect was sprung on the West. He despises India, even while sending fifty dollars a month to the family of his rescuer.

But his natural gift, so resonant in itself, extends exactly nowhere. He rarely reads, and when he does he confines himself to English murder mysteries. He is a man trapped in certain talents, incapable of growth, yet I envy him. They eat well, live well, and save thousands every year. They have no children, despite Susan's pleading, and they will have none until the child's full tuition from kindergarten through university is in the bank. While we empty our savings to make this trip to India. We'll hunt through bazaars and come up with nothing for our house. There is malevolence in our friendship; he enjoys showing me his New York, making the city bend to his wishes, extracting from it its most delicate juices. We discuss India this last night in America; aside from the trips to land a wife, he's never been back. And he won't go back, despite more pleading from Susan, until his parents die.

8

None of Deepak's restaurants tonight: it is steak, broiled at home. Thick steak, bought and cut and aged especially, but revered mainly for wet red beefiness. "Your meat *chagla*," he calls out from the kitchen, spearing it on his fork and holding it in the doorway, while Anjali, Susan, and I drink our gin and our son sips his Coke. A *chagla* is a side of beef. "Normally I use an onion, mushroom, and wine sauce, but don't worry—not tonight. Onions you will be having—bloody American steak you won't."

The time is near; two hours to lift-off. Then Deepak drives us to the airport because he says he enjoys the International Lounge, especially the Air-India lounge where any time, any season, he can find a friend or two whose names he's forgotten, either going back or seeing off, and he, Deepak, can have a drink and reflect on his own good fortune, namely not having to fly twenty-four hours in a plane full of squalling infants, to arrive in Bombay at four in the morning.

And so now we are sitting upstairs sipping more gin with Susan and Deepak, and of course two young men run over to shake his hand and to be introduced, leaving their wives, who are chatting and who don't look up. . . .

"Summer ritual," he explains. "Packing the wife and kids off to India. That way they can get a vacation and the parents are satisfied and the wives can boss the servants around. No wonder they're smiling. . . ." Looking around the waiting room he squints with disgust. "You'll have a full plane."

No Americans tonight, the lounge is dark with Indians. We're still in New York, but we've already left. "At least be glad of one thing," Deepak says. "What's that?" I ask. He looks around the lounge and winks at us. "No cows," he says.

No, *please*, I want to say, don't laugh at India. This trip is serious, for me at least. "Don't ruin it for me, Deepak," I finally say. "I may never go over again." "You might never come back either," he says. We are filing out of the lounge, down a corridor, and up a flight of stairs. Anjali and Deepak are in good spirits. Susan is holding our son, who wants another Coke.

". . . and the beggars," Deepak is saying, "*Memsahib*, take my fans, my toys, my flowers, my youngest daughter—"

"—then suddenly a leprous stump, stuck in the middle of the flowers and fans," says Anjali.

"Maybe that's India," I say, "in an image, I mean."

Deepak and Anjali both smile, as if to say, *yes, perhaps it is. Then again, perhaps it isn't. Maybe you should keep your eyes open and your mouth shut.* And then we are saying good-bye, *namaste-ing* to the hostess, and taking our three adjoining seats. India is still a day away.

9

"Listen for the captain's name," says Anjali. Need I ask why? Anjali's erstwhile intendeds staff the banks, the hospitals, the courts, the airlines, the tea estates of Assam and West Bengal. They are all well-placed, middle-aged, fair-complected, and well-educated Brahmins.

"D'Souza," we hear. An Anglo-Indian, not a chance.

"I heard that Captain Mukherjee is flying for Air-India now," she tells me. "He was very dashing at Darjeeling in '58, flying for the Air Force." Another ruptured arrangement.

There are times when I look at her and think: She, who had no men before me will have many, and I, who had those girls here and there and everywhere even up to the day I married but none after, will have no more, ever. All of this is somehow ordained, our orbits are conflicting, hers ever wider, mine ever tighter.

This will be a short night, the shortest night of my life. Leaving New York at nine o'clock, to arrive six hours later in London's bright morning light, the sunrise will catch us east of Newfoundland around midnight New York time. During the brief, East-running night two businessmen behind me debate the coming British elections. Both, as Indians, feel sentimental toward Labour. As businessmen they feel compromised. They've never been treated badly. Both, in fact, agree that too many bloody Moslems have been admitted, and that parts of England are stinking worse than the slums of Karachi or Bombay. Both will be voting Tory.

In the absurd morning light of 3 A.M. while the plane sleeps and the four surly sari-clad hostesses smoke their cigarettes in the rear, I think of my writing. Flights are a time of summary, an occasion for sweating palms. If I should die, what would I make of my life? Was it whole, or just beginning? I used to write miniature novels, vividly imagined, set anywhere my imagination moved me. Then something slipped. I started writing only of myself and these vivid moments in a confusing flux. That visionary gleam; India may restore it, or destroy it completely. We will set down an hour in London, in Paris, in Frankfurt, and even Kuwait—what does this do to the old perspectives? Europe is just a stop-over, Cokes in a transit room on the way to something bigger and darker than I'd ever imagined. Paris, where I survived two months without a job; Frankfurt where six years ago I learned my first German—*wo kann man hier pissen?* How will I ever return to Europe and feel that I've even left home? India has already ruined Europe for me.

10

From London we have a new crew and a new captain: His name is Mukherjee. Anjali scribbles a note to a steward who carries it forward. Minutes later he returns, inviting Anjali to follow him through the tiny door and down the gangway to the cockpit. Jealous Indians stare at her, then at me. And I, a jealous American, try to picture our dashing little captain, mustached and heavy-lidded, courting my wife when he should be attending to other things.

She stays up front until we land in Paris. My son and I file into the transit room of Orly, and there in a corner I spot Anjali and the captain, a small, dark, heavy-lidded fellow with chevroned sleeves a mite too long for his delicate hands.

"Hello, sir," he says, not reaching for my hand. He holds a Coke in one, a cigarette in the other. "Your wife's note was a very pleasant distraction."

"Nice landing," I say, not knowing the etiquette.

"Considering I couldn't find the bloody runway, I thought it was. They switched numbers on us."

"So," I say. "You're the fam—"

"No, no—I was just telling your wife: you think that I am Captain *Govind* Mukherjee formerly Group Captain Mukherjee of the IAF. But I am Sujit Mukherjee —regrettably a distant cousin—or else I would have met this charming lady years ago. I was just telling your wife that Govind is married now with three children and he flies out of Calcutta to Tokyo. I *knew* she was not referring to me in the chit she sent forward and I confess to a small deception, sir—I hope I am forgiven—"

"Of course, of course. It must have been exciting for her—"

"Oh, exciting I do not know. But disappointing, *yes*, decidedly. You should have seen the face she pulled spotting Sujit Mukherjee and not Govind—" Then suddenly he breaks into loud, heavy-lidded laughter, joined by Anjali and a gray-haired crew member standing to one side.

"This is my navigator, Mr. Misra," says the captain. "Blame him if we go astray."

"And this is our son, Ananda," I say.

"*Very* nice name, Ananda. Ananda means happiness."

"Are you the driver?" Ananda asks.

"Yes, yes, I am the *driver*," the captain bursts into laughter, "and Misra here is my wiper," and Misra breaks into high-pitched giggles. "Tell me, Ananda, would you like to sit with us up front and help drive the plane?"

"Would I have to go through that little door?"

"Yes."

"No," he says decisively. He holds my hand tightly, the captain and navigator bow and depart, and then we go for a Coke.

Somewhere out there, I remind myself, is Paris.

11

Back in the plane the purser invites me forward; Captain Mukherjee points to the seat behind him, the rest of the crew introduce themselves, a steward brings me lemonade, and the plane is cleared for leaving the terminal. Then an Indian woman clutching a baby bursts from the building, dashes across the runway waving frantically.

"Air-India 112—you have a passenger—"

"Stupid bloody woman," the captain says under his breath. "Air-India 112 returning for boarding," he says, then turns to me: "Can you imagine when we're flying the jumbo? Indians weren't meant for the jumbo jets."

Then the steward comes forward, explaining that the woman doesn't speak Hindi, English, or Tamil and that she doesn't have a ticket and refuses to take a seat. The only word they can understand is "husband." The captain nods, heavy-lidded, smiling faintly. "I think I should like a glass of cold water," he says, "and one for our passenger." He takes off his headphone, lights a cigarette. Turning fully around he says to me: "We have dietary problems. We have religious problems and we have linguistic problems. All of these things we prepare for. But these village women, they marry and their husband goes off to Europe and a few years later he sends for them. But they can't read their tickets and they won't eat what we give them and they sit strapped in their seats, terrified, for the whole trip. Then they fall asleep and we can't wake them. When they wake up themselves they think they're on a tram and they've missed their stop, so they tell us to turn around. London, Paris, Rome—these are just words to them. The husband says he will meet her in Paris—how is she to know she must go through customs? She can't even read her own language let alone *douane*. So she goes to the transit room and sits down and the husband she's probably forgotten except for one old photograph is tapping madly on the glass and when the flight reboards she dutifully follows all the people—"

"Captain, someone is talking to her."

"Fine, fine."

"She is to meet her husband in Paris."

"Did you tell her this is Paris?"

"She won't believe *me*, Captain. She wants you to tell her."

"Misra—take my coat and go back and tell her." To me he adds, "She wouldn't believe I'm the captain. Misra makes a very good captain with his gray hair. Where is my bloody ice water?"

"Yes, Captain. Right away, Captain."

Moments later we are taxiing down the runway, gathering speed and lifting steeply over Paris. The Seine, Eiffel Tower, Notre Dame, all clear from the wraparound windows. And, for the first time, my palms aren't sweating. Competence in the cockpit, the delicate fingers of Captain Mukherjee, the mathematical genius of Navigator Misra, the radar below, the gauges above. I settle back and relax. Below, the radar stations check in: Metz, Luxembourg, Rüdesheim, Mainz. I recognize the Rhine, see the towns I once hitchhiked through, and bask in the strangeness of it all, the orbits of India and my early manhood intersecting.

We descend, we slow, and Frankfurt appears. We turn, we drop still lower, slower, 200 miles per hour as we touch down. Everything perfect, my palms are dry again. It's been years since I felt such confidence in another person. The silence in the cockpit is almost worshipful.

The ground-crew chief, a gray-bearded Sikh, comes aboard and gives the captain his instructions for take-off, which the captain already knows. The weather conditions in Kuwait: 120° with sandstorms. Mukherjee nods, smiles. I ease out silently; *namaste-ing* to the captain and crew, thanking them all as they go about their chores.

12

Within an hour we are farther East than I've ever been. Down the coast of Yugoslavia, then over the Greek islands, across the Holy Land. What if the Israelis open fire? Those SAM missile sites, Iraqi MIGs scrambling to bring us down. Trials in Bagdad, hanging of the Jewish passengers. India is officially pro-Arab, an embarrassment which might prove useful.

This was the shortest day of my life. The east is darkening, though it's only noon by New York time. An hour later the stars are out; we eat our second lunch, or is it dinner? Wiener Schnitzel or lamb curry. Ananda sleeps; Anjali eats her curry, I my Wiener Schnitzel.

"After Kuwait things will deteriorate," she says. "The food, the service, the girls—they always do."

We've been descending and suddenly the seat-belt sign is on. Kuwait: richest country in the world. City lights in the middle of the desert, and an airfield marked by permanent fires. Corridors of flames flapping in a sandstorm and Captain Mukherjee eases his way between them. Sand stings the window, pings off the wings like Montreal ice.

"The ground temperature is forty-five degrees Centigrade" the hostess announces, and I busily translate: 113°F.

"The local time is ten p.m."

I whisper to Anjali, " 'I will show you fear in a handful of dust . . . '"

"Through passengers ticketed on Air-India to Bombay and New Delhi will kindly remain in the aircraft. We shall be on the ground for approximately forty-five minutes."

I can feel the heat through the plastic windows. Such heat, such inhuman heat and dryness. I turn to Anjali and quote again:

" 'Here is no water but only rock
   Rock and no water and the sandy road . . . '"

A ground crew comes aboard. Arab faces, one-eyed, hunched, followed by a proud lieutenant in the Kuwaiti uniform. These are my first Moslems, first Arabs. They vacuum around our feet, pick up the chocolate wrappers, clear the tattered London papers from the seats. It's all too fast, this "voyage out," as they used to call it. We need a month on a steamer, shopping in Italy, in Cairo, bargaining in the bazaars, passing serenely from the Catholic south to the Moslem heartland, thence to holy, Hindu India. The way they did it in the old novels. In Forster, where friendship and tolerance were still possible. No impressions of the Wasteland in a Forster novel. No one-eyed, menacing Arabs. But Forster is almost ninety, and wisely, he remains silent. The price we pay for the convenience of a single day's flight is the simple diminishment of all that's human. Just as Europe is changed because of India, so·India is lessened because of the charter flight. I'm bringing a hard heart to India, dread and fear and suspicion.

13

We are in the final hours over the Persian Gulf and the Arabian Sea, skimming the coast of Iran then aiming south and east to Bombay. Kuwait gave us children who play games in the aisles, who spill their Cokes on my sleeve. Captain Mukherjee, Misra, and the crack London crew ride with us as passengers; the new stewardess is older, heavier, and a recent blonde. No one sleeps, though we've set our watches on Bombay time and it is suddenly three o'clock in the morning.

"Daddy will be leaving for the airport now," says Anjali.

I've never met her parents. They've flown 1500 miles to meet us tonight, to see us rest a day or two before joining us in the flight back to Calcutta.

"The airport will be a shock," she says. "It always is."

"Anything to get off this plane."

Three-thirty.

Ananda has taken the window seat; he sits on his knees with his face cupped to the glass. He's been to India before, three summers before. He's forgotten his illness, remembers only an elephant ride and a trip to the mountains where he chased butterflies up the slopes.

Twenty minutes to India. I can feel the descent. Businessmen behind me agree on the merits of military rule.

"Ladies and gentlemen—"

The lights go on, a hundred seat belts buckle on cue. Lights suddenly appear beneath us. There are streets, street lamps, cars, bungalows, palm trees. My first palms since Florida—maybe I'll like it here—and we glide to a landing, our fifth perfect landing of the day.

Everyone is standing, pulling down their coats and baggage. I'd forgotten how much we carried aboard (three days ago, by the calendar): a flight bag of clothes for Ananda, camera equipment, liquor and cigars for my father-in-law, my rain hat and jacket, our three rain-coats and two umbrellas. We put on everything we can and then line up, facing first the rear and then the front, clutching our passports.

"Ladies and gentlemen, we have landed at Santa Cruz Airport in Bombay. The local time is four a.m. and the temperature is 33° Centigrade . . ."

"Over ninety," I whisper.

"It's been raining," she says.

As we file to the front and the open door, I can feel
the heat. My arms are sweating before I reach the lad-
der. An open bus is waiting to take us to the terminal.
No breeze, S.R.O. The duty-free bag begins to tear.

I follow our beam of light across the tarmac. A man
is sleeping on the edge of the cement, others have
built a fire in the mud nearby.

"Tea," Anjali explains.

Other thoughts are coming to me now: not the howl-
ing sand of Kuwait—*mud*. Not the empty desert—
people. Not the wind—*rain*. I want to scream: "*It's four
in the bloody morning and I'm soaking with sweat.
Somebody do something!*" Even in the open bus as we
zip down the runway there's no breeze, no relief. Anjali's hair, cut and set just before we left has turned
dead and stringy, her sari is crushed in a thousand folds.
This is how the world will end.

We are dropped in front of the terminal. Families are
sleeping on the steps. Children converge on our bus,
holding out their hands, making pathetic gestures to
their mouth. I have a pocket full of *centimes* and
pfennigs from this morning's stops, but Anjali frowns
as I open my hand. "They're professionals," she says.
"If you must give to beggars wait at least till you get to
Calcutta." They pull my sleeve, grab Ananda by the
collar of his raincoat, until a man behind us raises his
hand. "Wretched little scum," he mutters. They scatter
and I find myself half-agreeing.

We have come inside. Harsh lights, overhead fans.
Rows of barriers, men in khaki uniforms behind each
desk, desks laden with forms and rubber stamps. The

bureaucracy. Behind them the baggage, the porters squatting, the Customs, more men, more forms. Then the glass, the waiting crowd, the parents, the embraces, the right words, the corridors. *I'm not ready,* I want to scream, *turn this plane around.* I've stopped walking, the passports are heavy in my hand. I've never been so lost.

"Darling, what's the matter?" she asks, but she has already taken my hand, taken the passports, the declarations, and given me the flight bag in their place. Ananda stands before me, the beautiful child in his yellow slicker, black hair plastered to his forehead. I take his hand, he takes Anjali's, and I think again: *I'm not prepared,* not even for the answer which comes immediately: and if you're not, it says, who is?

Continent

of Strangers

A Love Story of the Recent Past

Frytha Magnusdottir, Icelandic stewardess, twisted her way down the narrow aisle, balancing a tray of empty cognac tumblers on the tips of her red, red fingernails. Keeler, bunched in a middle seat on the twenty-hour flight, devised a sudden tragic nosedive in which he—Viking in a yellow lifeboat—would corral Magnusdottir and the stock of cognac and drift in time to the shores of Greenland. Ah, Frytha, he thought, if only I were bolder, or had been blessed with a seat on the aisle.

"Dis is Captain Thorlaksen," came the Nordic lilt over the wheezing intercom, "in chust a minute, we be over the Hook of Holland . . ." Keeler, gazing down on the wrinkled purple of the English Channel, strained for the German equivalent that followed (never too early to begin the language), and caught only "Holland" in the middle of an endless sentence. The Austrian woman in the aisle seat chuckled, "Ach, so!" and winked. Keeler smiled. Then from the garbled French that followed, he learned what only the Continentals were to know: that liquor and tobacco in the Luxembourg Airport were duty-free. He thought of picking up a bottle of champagne to celebrate the upcoming nights with Janet, then discarded it. With the letter he had, champagne was superfluous. He felt himself reaching into his jacket for the letter, just to read it one more time.

"You catch what that guy said?" asked the brightly madrased boy from Cornell who had blocked most of the window since New York. Keeler, nearly disguised in somber corduroys (he could have been Canadian he felt), answered carefully, "We land in an hour."

"Cool."

Below, on a cloudless day, a bright brown "hook" indeed appeared, looking to Keeler like a miniature Cape Cod. Southeast lay their destination, Luxembourg, and just miles away across the Rhine: Germany. And in the *Ruhr Gebiet* of smoky cities, in Cologne, Janet was at this minute working, not suspecting he was just hours away.

The tissue-thin letter (*Luftpostleichtbrief!*) now rustled on his fingertips—the fragile, treasured thing: stained, wrinkled, and cloven along its major folds— it fell open lazily to its lone blue side, cramped with Janet's green handwriting. Though he knew every word, he treated himself to another reading.

"*My dear Paul,*" it began, and he melted. He remembered the first time he had noticed Janet Bunn: she had been mounting her bicycle in back of an Oberlin dorm, and he, driving by with friends, had turned when the driver whistled, "Jesus! Who's that?" To his surprise, Keeler knew the girl. They were in European Lit together, but had never talked. Hers was the build one notices suddenly, in an odd moment, after months of partial blindness.

A week later, she called him to ask about an assignment; after that they dated regularly. It was a spring romance of a senior year, between good students who had rarely dated. In two months they learned all they were capable of; they graduated with the sexual knowledge of sheltered freshmen. They talked of marriage more easily than of sex, and Keeler never doubted they would marry in time. "I'd like you to be the father of my children," Janet said, a sentiment that came embarrassingly close to summing him up. He *was* more father than lover, and he sensed that she—virginal, deep-bosomed, withdrawn—had simply been overlooked at Oberlin, where taste in women was often degraded. In Europe, he feared, they'd eat her alive. Kitten in a dog pound. They parted a week before graduation, intending to keep in touch, and always to trust in the inevitable.

Keeler chose Boston, a cleaner and purer city than any he'd known, but found despair. In six months he saw disorder enough for a lifetime of novels. Life was cheap among the Harvard drop-outs, and the dedicated life was a difficult thing to defend. In an apartment on lower Beacon Hill, he wrote at night and occasionally visited an older sculptress who shared his bath and kitchen. By day he worked in a bookstore, looking away as his acquaintances stole. In February two of his stories were taken by established quarterlies. In March Janet suddenly began to write to him. He responded brilliantly, spending long hours in a tearoom describing his delicate moods. In April, the letter he now was holding arrived. He'd checked his savings, done some borrowing, and taken a second job. And then in early July, he quit, packed, and took the earliest cancellation.

He looked down and read:

> *Köln*
> *20 April, 196–*

Dearest Paul:

I've thought and thought about us, Paul, and I've come to a decision. I'm sitting here tonight with Ingrid, in the room, drinking wine that her boyfriend brought from Sweden. I'm a little high tonight, and I know that I'll be very lonely tomorrow. She's decided to leave Köln and go back with him to Sweden right away. So I've been doing what spinsters do, I guess, reading letters from my old boyfriend. Maybe you didn't think you were writing love letters—I didn't even know you were—but tonight they seemed beautiful, Paul, really beautiful.

Anyway, maybe because she's Swedish, but also because she's too young to be sensible, she made a suggestion. At the time (a few hours ago—she's asleep now) I think I laughed at her, but she was serious. Now I am. I think I've been a fool. Have I?

I think so. I just woke Ingrid up and she said I've been one too. She asked me what you looked like, and I could barely remember, so I made you up, sort of rumpled and artistic, and very Easternish-sophisticated.

She wants to meet you, and so naturally she suggested that you come over for the summer.

She said also I've been a little idiot all along; she's eighteen and says that! I had so many expectations of the things that would happen to me in Europe, I admit it—I was daydreaming last year when we broke up, and I couldn't leave you and the States fast enough. The possibilities seemed infinite, but they've become impossibly narrow by now. I spend my days washing diapers in a laundry room underground with Italians who can't keep their hands off me. Three of my roommates have gotten pregnant and left—and I haven't even had the chance, really! (I'm not complaining exactly, just giving you the picture.)

Anyway, there's a solution, and I can only say this tonight and mail it, and maybe regret it tomorrow. Come over, Paul, I beg you. You can fly round-trip on Icelandic for $350 I think, and once you get here I can supply free room and food if you want to work here—and I've saved up 1000 D.M. wages anyway, just for the summer. I have to work till August 1st, and if you want to start grad school you'll have to go back by September, but that'll give us August together anyway, and you'll have the whole summer to tramp around, you lucky bum. I've seen Amsterdam and Berlin, and that's all. And everything'll be so perfect—Ingrid suggested that we come up to Sweden for August and stay in her cottage with Bengt and her, right on the beach. What do you say? Please write me right away, so I won't have time to become afraid.

> *All my love,*
> Janet

Keeler's hands were sweating as the continent at last rolled under the wing. It seemed they were already losing altitude, slicing nearer and nearer the neat little patches of lime-greenery, hatched with yellow roads. He looked at his watch: 4:30, teatime, but the sun was high in this northern latitude. Half the summer had slipped away while he saved for this trip. The waste still haunted him. Where was I, twenty-four hours ago, he wondered, New York, Boston, the Trailways bus in between? Ah, Boston, and a cold disgust crept up his legs. Thank God that chapter of his life was over; the job, the hideous room, the roach powder on the window sill. Especially the people. Even the sculptress and all her cats.

The night after receiving Janet's letter, he remembered, he had hustled over to Cambridge for a Bergman Festival. For the first time he thrilled more to Max Von Sydow's jovial language than to all of Bergman's effects. His spine now tingled and his breath came short, thinking of the adventure that awaited him. Europe at last, Janet his domain, the priceless experience—Paris, Rome, Cologne, the Alps—love!

And now, here he was.

His bag was being passed at Findel Field, Luxembourg, when Frytha Magnusdottir found him and delivered a letter. He glared a second at the intricate directions, all in German, that Janet had penned on the envelope. It hurt him that she should be so proficient. Then he tore it open.

The closing words struck him first: *Affectionately yours.* Grimly, without reading further, he claimed his new lightweight bag, now tagged in chartreuse with "LUX," and handed his passport across for its first European stamping.

He headed across the parking lot to the Icelandic offices to arrange for a return ticket, since he had come over on a one-way cancellation.

Inside, one of a battery of sweatered secretaries, gorgeous girls with short hair and high cheekbones, pushed pins on a board and offered him August 10, or September 15. He asked for a minute to decide, ducked out the door and scanned the letter.

Köln
July 5, 196–

Dear Paul:

So you're here after all. It's practically impossible to believe. I leave it to you how to get here from Luxembourg (trains are best), but if you want to visit France first, feel free. Just send a note first if you do. If you get here and I'm not in (I'll be in Berlin for a conference between July 9–12), call 4342 in Köln and ask for "Schwester Ann-Marie." Say it exactly like this: "Darf-ish-mit-Froyline-Janet-spreshen?" She'll put you up if I'm not here.

I don't know how to say the rest of this, Paul, now that you're here and I'm partly responsible. After I wrote you that first letter, I had misgivings (especially after Ingrid went back to Sweden), but I couldn't admit them in a letter. I hoped that you'd decide not to come, and I'd be left with my brave gesture. But I must have my freedom, Paul. If we travel together, very well, but if we find that we've changed, I must be free to act as though you weren't here. Please don't ask me to explain all this—it's just a feeling I have.

But welcome to Europe anyway, I'm sure you'll have the time of your life here, and maybe you'll find all the answers for yourself that I didn't. I'm looking forward to seeing you, please believe me.

Affectionately yours,

J.

Streams of tourists were headed to the office now, to change their bookings or leave messages. Secretaries, captains, Frytha and her stunning crew, were slamming doors and laughing in the windy corridor. Keeler went back into the office and surrendered his ticket. "Make it September," he said, "I can always come back earlier if I have to." And probably I will, he thought, stepping into the hallway, a very free and very lost young man.

Luxembourg to Frankfurt by train was easy enough; most of the travelers were American students and Europe had not yet broken through. Keeler sat alone, memorizing the warnings in German and French: *Ne jetez aucun objet . . . Keine Gegenstände aus dem Fenstern werfen.* He imagined someone entering the compartment at any moment and challenging him for a reservation. And as he watched the tracks eerily blend and branch under his window (they'd crossed into Germany by now) he feared that he had boarded the wrong train and at this moment was racing for Prague or Bucharest and would wake up in the morning in a sealed train, in the custody of an unfriendly power. He sat up, pulled down a folding table, and cradled his head in the nest of his arms, staring out the window into rural blackness.

From Frankfurt he was on his own. The station crawled with American soldiers, their whores and lackeys whom he dodged. He found a *Wechselstube* and cashed his first twenty dollars. Wordlessly, except for "Köln" and one finger raised, he bought a ticket on a midnight local.

Throughout the night split-second connections were made in the larger Rhine cities—Wiesbaden and Mainz, where soldiers again formed the only crowd—Bingen, Koblenz (clean and desolate stations where decrepit conductors in high-peaked Wilhelmite caps and red Prussian sashes waved the *Zug* on), moving down the Rhine, not even slowing at the nameless hamlets, stopping at cities vaguely familiar from war movies, or Thomas Mann: Andernach, Rheineck, Sturzig, Remagen. A long cold dawn began, gray and feeble over the ridges across the Rhine. In the empty stations, benches advertised the local papers: *Frankfurter Allgemeine* bowing to the *Mainzer Zeitung*, which yielded at last to the *Bonn Morgenblatt*. At seven o'clock came Bad Godesberg, where a mighty crowd of ebullient businessmen shoved their way aboard, jamming the *Abteil* with a cheery gibberish. The smell of morning cigarettes and coffee made his stomach ache for food. Then, moments later, came Bonn. Bonn! He had dreamed of a mighty city, a stately capitol perched on a bluff, yet from the train he spotted nothing but workers and housewives chatting on the corners waiting for the lights to change. And at last, twenty minutes later, the train rolled into a tiny suburban station tagged simply, KŌLN-SŪD, and his nerves nearly snapped with the nearness of it all.

Smiling as though he understood, but no longer confident of his disguise, he pushed with his seatmates out of the compartment and into the aisle, peering out the windows that pulled down and let the cold air in. German air. For an anxious quarter-hour the lesser Cologne stations crept past, each surrendering its horde of commuters. Then, magically, they came upon a high bridge spanning the Rhine, and through the gray mist rising from the water, he made out the giant spires of the mighty cathedral, dominating a low, hostile skyline.

Minutes later, inside a monster terminal that vaulted thirty tracks, he stood at last on solid concrete. The plaque overhead entranced him: KŌLN HBf. At the far end of the terminal, by the set of exits (*Ausgang!*), the famous Kölnischwasser was advertised in dull pre-war paint, in the Bad Old Script. Germans raced about him, knocking against his flight bag and cursing like New Yorkers. But he savored the slow walk to the steps, humming as he stepped, "I'm here, Janet, I'm here."

Downstairs he put his bag in a *Handgepäck*, then sat at the short-order counter. He breakfasted on the two items he recognized from the menu: *Bier* and *Brötchen*, ashamed to order in English and disturb the somber slurping gentlemen who had made room for him so somnambulantly when he sat down. Down the main corridor, now clogged with rushing well-dressed businessmen, he made out flower shops and grocery stalls, and out on the street, the black bulk of the Cathedral just across the square. Then he took out a pocket notebook and jotted down all the words he'd learned.

Sleep was nearing at last, after he finished the tall warm beer, and he realized he needed rest, before he could bargain with Janet's freedom. According to her letter, she'd be back tomorrow.

He found the Information Desk, which was just opening, and asked where he could find a cheap room. His second European girl, a brunette with brick-red cheeks and crackling blue eyes, located a room nearby for five marks, $1.25. And to satisfy a keen but diminishing desire, he asked her her name, which she surrendered, he swore, with a full understanding of a tourist's and lover's jumbled emotions.

"Monika," she said, and even asked him his.

2

He slept without dreaming in a bitterly cold bed, under a single airy quilt, and awoke in the late afternoon, roused from sleep by the rapping of rain on the skylight above. Unrefreshed, head still dull, he longed to sleep some more, but felt the urgency of reaching Janet, now that an ocean no longer intervened. His summer was short enough. Downstairs he found the telephone, checked Janet's directions, then persuaded the manager to place the call.

"Darf-ish-mit-Froyline-Janet-spreshen?" Keeler blurted when a woman's voice answered. She responded in a slushy German that seemed to end in a question, while he pleaded that he spoke no German. "Fräulein Janet!"

"Ach, *so! Ya*-net . . ." came the sudden enlightenment from the other end. "*Nicht hier*. Not here." Then came a muffled rush of commands, and a new voice.

"Hallo? Mr. Keeler is it? This is here Sister Ann-Marie. We have been expecting you. Janet is to Berlin, but she is back tomorrow. We billet you here, and we have place in the laundry for working. Board a tram in the Bahnhofsplatz number twenty-seven. Disboard in the next-to-the-last station. There you transfer to a number fifty-two and disboard at the end station. It is called *Westhausen*. Where you transfer is called Platz Friedrich-Ebert. When you disboard, then you walk up a hill which is Paradestrasse, to a small Platz. There you see two flags—the American and the Cherman. You come for dinner, ja?"

"That's very kind, sister. But I've already paid for a room in the city. I'd feel a little out of place if Janet weren't there."

"Nonsense," snapped Sister Ann-Marie, "we're one under in the laundry room."

"Well—sure," said Keeler. "But what do I say on the tram to get off and all?"

"Say this: *Kernen-Zee-mir-zagen-vo-ish-umsteigen-muss*? That is for the first time. For getting off is the same thing, but you say *aus-steigen*, not *umsteigen*. We expect you in an hour. Eating time is six o'clock."

He stood an hour on the cranky little streetcar, jammed between commuters going home, embarrassed by his bag that blocked the aisle and cost him thirty pfennig *Zuschlag*. Finally, in an area of wet meadows behind rows of cottages, the trolley came to its loop. It was a lovely setting: heavily wooded hills, steep pastures, colorful cottages, far from the feeling of a dirty city. He crossed the road and took a steep incline to a ridge, where another road intersected, forming a little square. Ahead lay a low modern building with two drenched flags clinging to the shafts by the door. The building overlooked open pastures and a lazy trail. This is more like it, he thought.

Once inside, he asked a squat middle-aged nurse for Schwester Ann-Marie, and discovered it was her. He was led down a glistening hall to a flight of stairs.

"So, Mr. Keeler, we are happy you are with us. Come," she commanded, and he followed her down the stairs to a noisy laundry room. Half a dozen swarthy men and two attractive girls with boyishly cut hair were feeding soiled diapers and sheets into steaming vats, rinsing, then wringing them. The steam was sweet with urine and soap; the men didn't look, the girls smiled but said nothing. He followed the nurse through the laundry room, past a puddled shower stall, into a bunk room.

"You are used to sleeping like this? Is here where our men sleep that works out there. *Italiener*. So." He set the bag down at the foot of a made-up bunk, then followed her back upstairs.

"Down in that room you was in is where Janet works, sometimes. You can stay here and have all food, as long as you want. Pay is one hundred marks a month."

"That's very nice," he said. "Ah—where does Janet sleep?"

"Up here, with the girls you seen, Hannalore and Traudl. She asked to live here with them after Ingrid went back to Sweden. These girls, Mr. Keeler—" The nurse dropped her voice to a noisy whisper. "They both have babies here that was born from soldier fathers. American soldiers. Swedes—" She waved a thick pink arm, "Swedes isn't good for this work. They take it too personal. But your Janet—she is a very good worker."

Keeler nodded.

"When the bell rings, then means supper is ready. Being Monday we have blood sausage and cheese. I hope you like, Mr. Keeler?"

"I'm sure I will."

"So, we see you at dinner. Janet is back in the morning. Getting up time is six-thirty. *Guten Appetit, Herr Keeler.*"

The sausage, he discovered, was the color and consistency of congealed blood, barely stomachable. He downed instead several slices of pebbly bread, loaded with cheese. The Italians at his table watched him carefully, laughing as they chattered. Certainly, he felt, they were talking of Janet, and of the times (how often, where, what else?) they had laid their hands upon her. With a sudden sharp jealousy, he remembered the marvelous plumpness of her breasts, and the few occasions he had held them. He was ashamed that he couldn't remember, exactly, what she looked like.

Later, while his bunk-mates played cards in the laundry room, Keeler lay awake, staring at the ceiling, then

at the tags on his blanket. *Hand-Wasch.* A cottage by
the sea, love-making before a fire, Ingrid of the ashen
tresses, he smiled—my Europe?

He had been rinsing diapers for three hours the next
morning before Sister Ann-Marie beckoned him from
the stairwell. Traudl, who knew some English, tittered,
"Janet's back!" as Keeler dropped the diapers, rinsed his
hands, and galloped to the nurse's side.

"So. Someone is waiting for you *hinauf.*"

His breath deserted him; he watched his trousers
mount the stairs, feeling nothing in his legs.

"I will leave you for the afternoon," she said, just
outside her office door. "She is in there, O.K.?"

"Thank you," he whispered. He wiped his sweating
hands on his corduroys, took a breath, and opened the
door. *Yes,* his mind flashed—that's Janet! Janet not as he
barely remembered her, but a woman now, long-haired,
slimmer, in a suede jacket and sandals. Her feet were
dirty. He had just an instant of objectivity, and in that
instant he reminded himself that Janet was not really a
pretty girl. But what did it matter? The distance he had
navigated! And the instant had passed, and all judgment
blurred. Her dimples were there, her eyes still soft and
brown, her skin tanned, but with rosy cheeks; she was
perfection. She looked up, and smiled shyly.

"I'm sorry I wasn't here to meet you."

"Janet, you're looking great. *Great!*" He took her
hand, then kissed her forehead, which was all she offered. Something he had forgotten about those months
at Oberlin was suddenly resurrected: they had never
talked easily together.

"So. They have you working downstairs."

"What a hole," he laughed. "And those characters down there are awful."

"They're not so bad. The Italians are a lot of fun, and I like Hannalore very much. Traudl's a flirt. She's sleeping with one of the Italians."

He sat on the arm of the leather chair, circling her with his arm. She was blonder than he remembered (perhaps the ammonia fumes had bleached her hair?), and a little less buxom. He kissed her on the cheek, lingering for a response that came very lightly.

"I don't want to . . . just yet, Paul," she apologized. "It's been a year after all. We'll have time later—it's just that I'm not sure of my emotions yet . . ." She looked up at him, then frowned. "Don't look at me like that. You make me feel like I'm on an auction block."

"Janet, I didn't know what to think after getting that letter at the airport yesterday. That wasn't much of a greeting."

"I meant it, Paul, every word. I must have my freedom. I must be able to do what I want, as though you weren't there. If our interests coincide, and if we find we want to be together, then it'll be lovely. But if it's going to be a test of wills, or if you have mistaken notions about what I meant, then it's best to settle it right here so we don't ruin the summer."

"I didn't think I could misinterpret that first letter, Janet. It said very clearly that you wanted me with you in Sweden this summer. Janet, I *know* that letter, I'm ashamed to say how many times I've read it . . ."

She laughed, and rested her head on his arm. "Paul,

I think I *may* love you. It's just that I didn't promise anything." She curled her feet under her skirt. "It's just that this year's been tough on me. You don't know what this kind of living can do, six days a week with babies, not getting out, not having anyone to talk to—I was terribly lonely when I wrote that letter. Ingrid even was worrying about me. There were ugly scenes with my other roommates when their boyfriends kept calling. And I was right in the middle of it—but I wasn't really in it at all. I had to make a choice—would I be like those other girls, or would I respect myself enough to keep on working?"

Her voice was even, reasoned, and though he didn't see where he fitted in, he was convinced the year had been just as hard on her. Janet's hands were in her lap, directly under him; he noticed the bitten nails, the frayed cuticles spotted with tiny scabs.

"I'm all mixed up," she went on in a voice much higher and straining for breath. "What I came over for I didn't find. I'm talking about rewards, spiritual things, whatever I used to call them. The only good thing I've done is become responsible to these people, and to the children. They trust me, and they look up to me. But . . . well, Paul—" Then her voice cracked, and Keeler was horrified that he had brought her to tears so quickly. "Every friend I've made in Germany is an unwed mother," she sobbed, "think how I'd feel if we went off and did it right away and if anything happened. Think about it. Think about *me*."

Keeler dug for a handkerchief, and dropped it on her lap. He was ashamed, despite his innocence, for pressing something he didn't yet desire himself. "I agree to everything," he said. "I'll always think about you first." They sat silently for several minutes, then Janet suggested a tour before lunch.

She led him out the back, past the nursery and half a dozen mulatto toddlers who cried as she brushed by. They walked a while along the narrow road that followed the crest of the ridge, then they swooped down a steep path that cut through emerald pastures into a dark woods. Young couples were wading in a stream, hundreds of feet below them, and shouting up merrily. Keeler seemed to understand every word.

"Isn't it glorious?" Janet called, laughing, as she ran down the path, leaping over roots, sending a heavy spray back with each bough she brushed. The leaves beneath their feet were wet and springy. Keeler, winded, aching, and very happy, finally wrestled her to the ground, just in sight of a relic castle perched on a distant ridge several miles down the valley.

"*Ottos Schloss,*" she gasped. "We'll walk to it Sunday if you want. It's a famous landmark around here."

How foolish I was to worry, he thought, suddenly very conscious of being young and willful, and in love. He held her close; she brought his hand to her breast.

"How green was my valley," he said.

He toiled the next day at the first vat, with the very dirty diapers. Occasionally, Janet would come down for an armload of cleaned clothes and offer a few words of (what else?) derision. The Italians were respectfully quiet, and Hannalore spoke to him in simple German, telling him, he felt, what an outstanding woman Janet was.

Sunday's hike to Otto's Castle settled the major problem in his future: there *would* be an August for them in Sweden. With Janet supplying the necessary German for buying tickets and beer, he played the role of sophisticated lover, the type who journeys over borders courting women in their languages. On the walk back, they opened a bottle of Moselle and sipped slowly, stretched in the sun by a natural dam. It reminded them of pastures they had found a spring before, in Ohio. But Janet, reading every gesture accurately, said at the beginning, "I'm not ready yet, Paul." They talked over the possibilities of his staying on at the Quaker home for the next three weeks, till vacation time. They decided he should see more of Europe rather than wait and scrub for their one-day weekends. Nothing would ripen, they thought, with both of them working. They would meet at the youth hostel in Copenhagen, three weeks later.

The next morning, armed with a list of work-camps, French hostels, and German Student Agencies, Keeler took the tram across the city to the Autobahn entrance and thrust a thumb in the direction of Paris. He was there by late that night, humming "Milord" all the way.

Three days later he was sitting on a bench in the Latin Quarter, near the UNESCO Auberge where he stayed. New sandals had weakened his arches and begun to shred his heel. He'd walked everywhere, ridden to the top, or bottom, of every monument. That afternoon, resting on the bench with a German-French phrasebook and a hunk of bread at his side, watching the dozens of lovely young French girls in yellow sunglasses and brave pastels pass by, he realized that there would be nothing for him in Europe without Janet at his side.

God, I'm a tourist, he thought, the one thing he'd vowed not to be. There seemed to be no way of meeting the people, of seeing the necessary things. He felt the old Boston existence opening again to take him in, his pastoral dreams falling apart. Hating himself for it, he wished for the rapid passage of three more weeks.

Idiot! he slammed his fist on the bench. Writer, lover, *man*—an empty tankard won't fill itself. *Go!* He went to a student cafeteria, bought wine and yoghurt, and swore that night he'd really begin his summer in Europe.

Place Pigalle—one place where an American can encounter France—was still dusky at 7:30, not jammed, not festive. He strode down the boulevard, pausing at each corner to check the girls up the sidestreets. He walked the compound four times, checking new faces, avoiding the old. He must be careful, he told himself; as with de Sade or any adolescent, the wrong girl could finish him for good. Finally he settled on a corner by a peddler hawking watches for the serious business of making a choice. Janet, who had been with him all week in conversations, clung tightly to his conscience.

Isn't it enough, she whispered, that I supply lodgings, that *I* remain faithful?

Is this really necessary, considering the risks, the embarrassment, perhaps? he wondered.

What embarrassment?

What if . . . what if you screw up. It can be done—first trip to a prostitute, rushed, the language barrier . . .

Language barrier?

The cost? VD?

Now, just emerging from a doorway and taking her place beside a six-foot blonde, was his girl. Short and youthful, in a beige suit; a convent girl lost in the city. He counted twenty-five francs and headed across the street. She saw him coming and turned away—demurely —into two Americans coming the other way, balding fraternity boys in madras shorts. She smiled at them. Keeler had his money out. So did the boys, and they got to her first.

"Forty francs for two quickies?"

"Nevair!"

"Twenty-five for one?" Keeler put in.

"We seen her first, buddy."

She leaned against the door, bored.

"We like your looks. Make it, say, forty-five and that's tops."

"Feefty for you both and I not charge for the room."

"It's a deal." Each took a hand and she led them up the street three doors, while Keeler pocketed the pastel wad of bills. He was shaking after coming so close. Fear had shriveled his very desire, and he knew now what terrible shame would have gripped him in that room, where by now the two Phi Gams were folding their clothes neatly on a chair. He walked down the boulevard one more time, smiling at the girls who guessed his problem now, and puckered their lips at him as he passed.

The internationalists back at UNESCO were staging a dance when he returned. He was in high spirits, for a man who had developed cold feet on Place Pigalle. A red-haired Israeli girl taught him a *hora* step in private, but he balked at joining her on the floor. "A stumbler at the dance," he said, pointing at himself, but she said she did not understand. But still, he felt twenty-five francs richer, and secure in his limitations. There would still be August; until then he was freer than most, just to observe. That evening as he watched the dancers enjoying themselves so unself-consciously, he took comfort in a new sensation: for him, Europe promised something different, something quite beyond twenty-five francs admission. His was a Europe of shrunken dimensions, and he was no bold discoverer. He was a writer, a creator; he would learn to satisfy himself with that.

3

The problem, he knew, was this: college had taught them both that the natural state for unmarried couples was virginity. If arousal persisted, a young man married; if not, he studied. Unmarried women did selfless and constructive things, voyaging with Quakers or the Peace Corps to continents in need. Always the grim little world of the good people. But in Boston he'd encountered a grimmer world, being the responsible half of shared apartments, stuck with the spill-over of messy lives. In his last months he'd taken a room in a transient hotel, eaten one meal a day in a tinkling little tearoom.

At twenty-two he resembled the bookstore clerks of forty-years' standing, the shufflers and coughers, the bachelors of fifty with a gleam in their eye. He applied to graduate schools, and then went to Europe for one last chance.

He knew precisely the sort of man he wanted to be and the knowledge brought him pain. Oberlin had shielded him from women of the world, those with whom the terror of success might rival the bitterness of defeat. Keeler pictured the girls of Paris as collectors of men, each of those slender nymphets of the Latin Quarter, discarding men like empty bottles. Even the pale, stooped girls in bookstores were mistresses to gray-haired bankers in camel's hair coats, free on weekends to try a stranger. He wasn't choosy, he'd take a stray who could use his protection. He walked the late evening streets in the heavy summer rains, stopping for a *vin rouge* every few blocks, hoping for a girl who could spot his needs, for an impulsive countess to tap the window of a sleek Citroën, summoning him into the back seat for a midnight run to the Costa del Sol.

Under Cinzano umbrellas he sat with Cokes and foreign papers: Israeli, Swedish, German, eyes slavering over the tops of the page. *To be here with Janet!* To be sitting here with the girl he loved, hoarding a table on the Champs Élysées, ignoring each other as each of them read. Knowing simply that she was there. That afternoon, that evening, they would return to their room with wine and a *baguette*, and make love on a narrow student bed, in a whitewashed room with political posters on the wall. Then back to their books, their movies, their fervent walks with a *Guide Michelin,* and memories freshened by the novels of Céline.

But Oberlin had not taught the art of quiet confidence in the company of women. He was a retarded twenty-two in the city of dreams, where mistakes in love were fatal. For him, no countesses, no sheltered girls who might find him exotic. Paris was a city of the crudest, most poignant promise for a would-be writer. A city that no one stalked alone without the most terrible admissions about himself.

He passed the two weeks hitchhiking around Normandy visiting cathedrals, then back to Germany via the Low Countries, then over the Autobahn to Hamburg and north. Janet was to meet him in Copenhagen for the trip to Sweden. He spent a day in Lübeck, visited Buddenbrooks House and walked the streets that Tonio Kröger had known. He felt restored, again a creator. William Faulkner had just died, Hermann Hesse died on the day he crossed into Denmark. Land of Kierkegaard and Hans Christian Andersen, and Keeler skipped through the streets of Odense and Copenhagen like a sly and seductive Danny Kaye.

4

They hitched together up the eastern flank of Sweden, past whitewashed farms where Holstein cattle nibbled grass to the edge of the Baltic; to Västervik, where they boarded a steamer for the five-hour crossing.

They stood on the bridge, watching whitecaps flash

against the bow. It was cold but sunny, and he shivered with excitement. Lined up beside them were other young couples, all straining for a glimpse of Gotland. Tall, tanned girls with long blond hair, in slacks and revealing sweaters, wearing wooden clogs. The Swedish men, next to their women, seemed to Keeler frail and ineffectual.

"What does Ingrid look like?" he asked.

"Pretty," Janet shrugged. "By our standards anyway."

She ducked down to the powder room to fix her hair an hour before they were in Visby harbor; he, stirred by the crisp wind, stayed topside and scanned the horizon. Finally, through the purple and blue of the sea, the sky, and the tandem set of Swedish flags, he made out the pale yellow cliffs and lavender hills of Gotland. Janet, with her bag, and her hair piled high, stood at his side for the last half hour with her hand in his.

As the ship backed to the dock, she picked out Ingrid, with Bengt (they presumed), and another girl at her side. Ingrid from a distance was tall, blond, wore sunglasses, slacks, and a red and white striped sweater. The other girl, much shorter and a little tubby, wore black slacks and a turtleneck black sweater. Her hair was very short, and nearly white. Bengt, in a light blue jacket, was Ingrid's height and bearded. The Americans waved but no one responded. Not until Janet bolted down the gangway to her did Ingrid take off her sunglasses and wave. They embraced, while the others turned to Keeler who hurried down with both bags.

"Paul—this is Ingrid!"

"Finally," he said. She drew him close and kissed him on the cheek. "I'm responsible for bringing you here—I hope you won't regret it," she laughed. She had no accent, not even the stage-Swedish that he hoped for. With a broad smile—a mite too broad—her face seemed more playful than perfect. Her shoulder-length hair was the color of fresh butter, and her eyes—blue as the Swedish flag—sparkled behind blond lashes.

"This is *my* friend, Bengt Ahlssen," she said, repeating Keeler's name to Bengt. "He is very sorry that he speaks no English." Bengt thrust a thick tanned forearm at Keeler and said, "Very happy," then turned to Janet, took her hand, and said it again. Though his hair was blond, the beard was black and wiry. Keeler read with awe the crest on his jacket: three gold crowns and a scroll: *XVIIOLYMPIADEN.*

"And this is Aino," Ingrid went on.

"Your sister?"

"No, no—she worked this summer in Visby and will be staying with us another week or so. Aino is a Finn."

She had the rosy cheeks of a child, and hair so white and fine the pink line of her scalp was faintly visible. A strand of pungent smoke curled up her arm from her cupped hand. When she brought the cigarette to her lips, Keeler noticed her fingers were deeply stained. "I have been waiting to meet you," she said, turning to Keeler. Then she exclaimed, "Americans, I love your language!"

They piled into Ingrid's Volvo and were off for the cottage, several miles south of Visby on the beach road.

It was a perfect shelter for lovers, under a bower of pines, heated only by an open fire, furnished in wickerwear with dozens of pillows. Janet and Keeler were assigned the bedroom with its twin cots and heavy quilts.

Bengt and Ingrid chose the floor, arranging themselves in sleeping bags before the fire. Aino took the sofa, and would bundle herself in coats and blankets. For cooking there were two butane burners, and for refrigeration, an icy spring nearby. Kerosene lanterns and the fireplace supplied the only light.

After dinner Keeler and Bengt were sent to the beachhouse for extra blankets. It was August 3, in the early evening, but already a chilly autumn had descended. The ocean, said Bengt in German, lay just over a ridge of dunes beyond the beachhouse, where a raw sun was setting through leaden clouds. "*Öd und leer das Meer*," quoted Keeler, who'd suddenly lost all feeling for the sea.

Then they sat around the fire after eating, talking and singing, drinking coffee until their nerves tingled and their breath came short. Janet, the folksinger, had brought her guitar to Europe but rarely had the opportunity to play. She compensated now by leading all the new songs she'd learned on *Liederabend,* and the old ones, from religious camps she'd been to as a child. Bengt and Keeler knew no songs, and couldn't sing; they sat silently, stilled by their various barriers. The girls sang well together.

"Perhaps one night Paul Keeler will read us his stories," Aino said, hours after she'd been forgotten on the sofa.

"I don't think I could read them aloud," he said, hoping the others would insist. No one did.

The conversation smoldered for hours, then finally died. Keeler grew drowsy, despite the caffein-stretching of his nerves. He leaned back on Janet's hot denimed leg while Bengt poked the coals with a straw to relight his pipe. How can we graciously retire, Keeler wondered. He imagined the iciness of the bedroom, the warmth of their bodies under a quilt. He shivered, though his face was burning. Janet had run out of songs, and Aino of song suggestions. They had come down to high-class show tunes before Janet's fingertips cracked.

"I have been thinking what would be perfect now," Aino burst in after Janet yawned, "especially for our guests." She sat up.

"Hot chocolate!" Keeler interjected.

"*After*, Paul Keeler. But first, sea-bathing! Who will go with me?"

"In the ocean?" asked Janet.

"Of course. It is a custom."

"Tomorrow, in the sun," Keeler shuddered.

"They're Americans, Aino," said Ingrid. "They might not want to." But Aino was already explaining her idea to Bengt in Swedish. He nodded, saying softly, "yo . . . yo . . ."

"I want to!" Janet cried. "Do we need . . . anything?"

Ingrid giggled. Aino found a lantern, and soon Ingrid had collected sufficient towels for the dip. Much too quickly, it seemed to Keeler, they were jogging down the over-grown path, past the beach-house and over the dunes. The wind was blunt and cruel; the sea roared out of darkness. At the last ridge of dunes they came to a deserted coast-guard bunker, with the remains of several fires scattered behind. A minute later Aino was stripped

[111]

to her black bra and panties while the others slapped their hands and stamped the ground.

"Well?" Aino called. Bengt unzipped his Olympic jacket, then peeled his sweater off. Keeler felt his own body grow white and soft in comparison, as it might on a parachute drop. Aino dashed down the slope, a tiny milk-white nude under the frigid moon.

"Come on, Paul," Janet urged.

"Don't be crazy," he hissed.

"The others are. It looks like fun."

"They're used to it. It's their custom."

Ingrid approached, still in her slacks, a towel draped around her naked shoulders. "Are you two coming?"

Keeler sat and clamped his arms around his knees. Janet glanced at him, then at Ingrid, who now unbuttoned her slacks.

"We're strangers," he said.

"This is Sweden," said Ingrid.

Keeler stared at her; his hostess now in panties and towel, carelessly draped. Pale, firm, her flesh was an embarrassing delight. What a favored man I am, he suddenly thought, to hear of this girl in a letter from six thousand miles, and now have her before me, a friend, naked.

He watched.

"I'll be with you in a minute," Janet decided, already out of her jeans and sweater, her back to him.

"You must run to the water and not hesitate a moment—or else you might get chilled," Ingrid advised her. "Paul, you're not coming?"

"I'm too cold," he muttered, clenching his teeth. Ingrid wrapped the towel tightly so only the tips of her panties showed. Then she turned and shed them. Janet now was bare. Suddenly a bundle of clothes dropped from the bunker roof. Keeler glanced up, to stare at Bengt who was peering down.

Janet jumped and covered herself, then she and Ingrid dashed to the beach.

"You-go-swim-Paul?" Bengt called down from a push-up position.

"No." *Me stay. You go.*

"Paul . . ." Bengt's voice was soft, pronouncing his name as a foreign word. "Paul . . . *es ist Schweden.*"

"It's Sweden," Keeler repeated. Bengt smiled and nodded sharply. Then he flipped to the sandbank at the bunker's side, shed his underwear like an Olympic track star, and sprinted to the others out of sight beyond the curve of dunes.

Sweden, his mind cried, astonished that these hard and heedless people were exactly as he once had hoped. He walked to the bunker face and gazed out to sea, till the dark and distance blended. *Es ist Schweden.*

I wanted this, he thought. For other people, I wanted it. For Janet and me to watch them. Janet, Janet, I'm twenty-two years old, look at me—I'm no elf. No little troll. *Troll nur in Norwegen gibt . . .* Look at yourself. We're old, we're soft, we're stumblers. It's war between us and them. We'd flop around on the sand like two beached whales.

Half the sky, he noticed now, was dull with clouds; the rest, shrinking rapidly, was imprinted with stars, coldly brilliant. Even as he watched, the moon was overtaken with haze, then obliterated. Lightning flashed behind the bulk of thunderclouds, revealing a storm horrendously close. Did these Swedes know their Baltic? Tonight the sea was the breeder of undertows, swamping waves and sudden ledges. A dull surf reflecting a patch of moon, the only light.

I am weak, he thought. Then, more defiantly; *Do it my way, Janet. In words, by a fire.* Words by a fireplace; let me read to you, and you will melt in my arms.

Thunder rolled, lightning crashed nearer. The first drops of icy rain splashed him in the face. My baptism, he thought. He gathered the piles of clothes in his arms, then waited, growing damp under the bunker's narrow eaves.

The torrent had subsided to an insistent drizzle when Aino, chased by Bengt, came laughing into view with Ingrid and Janet, gasping for breath, just behind. Keeler dispensed their clothes, then suddenly faced the sea as they dressed. "*Tak* Paul," said Aino. "*Magne tak.*" Rain and spray lashed his face; in one ear came the shriek of wind and surf, in the other the sound of his friends, giggling as they pulled their clothing on.

"I've never been so cold in all my life!" Janet cried.

"Thank you for minding our clothes, Paul Keeler," Aino called. "Now," she announced, "now we run back. You will be our lightbearer, Paul Keeler."

Inside, rainwater had doused the embers. The Swedes, miraculously warmed by the swim, methodically rebuilt the fire, while Janet dived into bed fully dressed and Keeler hunted in his bag for the batch of promised stories.

"I will read these tonight," Aino promised as he handed them to her. She lay pink and contented, rubbing her hair with a giant towel. "If you are cold, I will make hot chocolate," she said.

"Thank you, but we're anxious to get some sleep."

"We don't get up before ten o'clock usually," Ingrid called as she waved in at Janet. Then Keeler closed the door and they were silent in the rhythm of an autumn rain. The room was so dark he couldn't guess where the window was, or which wall he faced.

"You have to get out of those wet things," he whispered. She hadn't budged from the corner of her bed. A few seconds later, after he had settled himself in bed, her quilt rustled and she dashed for the throw rug by the dresser where she had laid out her bedclothes hours before. A sliver of firelight now strayed under the door; flickering, unreliable, it outlined Janet as she began undressing. He stared, expectant and shivering. From the living room came giggles, and Bengt's full laughter. The fire died down, Keeler strained harder, but could only hear the unsnapping of her jeans; the sparks as she peeled the sweater over her head; the fresh snap of elastic as her panties slid down her legs. So faintly it was painful, he made out her arms through the furry darkness—he reached for them and slammed his hand on the foot of his bed. Then, only by sounds and a teasing glow, came the tenderest moment of all: the unhooking of the bra, the smile that would come over her as she set her bra aside . . .

"Janet, come to me."

"I can't. I'm getting undressed," she whispered. Soon

the cabin jiggled with her racing back to bed. The beds were on opposite sides of the room, the longest ten feet he'd ever seen.

"Come over here a while—it would be warmer for you."

"All right." Her compliance, it seemed to him, was far too easy, as though she might be joining him merely for the warmth. She settled in a ball at his side. Her body hardened with cold; he ran his hands under her pajama tops down her trembling back.

"Janet, Janet," he soothed, and she drew nearer, piercing his feet with thrusts of her toes. Her skin was clammy. There was, that moment, he thought, not a drop of understanding in her for the feelings he had to deliver. It was like looking deep into the eyes of a child, or a beloved pet, or maybe just a dolphin, and hoping to communicate by love, or intentions, alone.

"Janet," he cried, seizing her hardened breast. "Janet, let me love you."

"Pleas-se . . . I'm not able. Don't force me."

"Straighten out, lie against me." He pulled her stiffened body to the area he had warmed, by backing himself to the wall.

"Thank you," came her distant voice. His face was dampened by her piled-up hair, now sticky with salt and fragrant with the beach.

"You'll stay with me tonight?"

"No." He waited for something more, but she had finished. He pulled her closer, and anxiously began pulling the bobby pins out of her hair. He kissed her, and she turned away.

[116]

Then suddenly she turned to him, her forehead hot on his chin. "Why wouldn't you go swimming tonight?" she charged. "You put me in an impossible position—"

"Janet—"

"It felt very good, once you got used to it. Coming back was cold, that's all."

"Well, what difference does it make? I'm not the type. I get shy before strangers without any clothes on. Even if I'd done it, it wouldn't be *me* doing it, understand? I'm not myself in a crowd." He dug his fingers under the halter of her pajamas, where a sudden pocket of cool skin was now inviting.

"Paul—I'm not in the mood."

"Maybe next time I'll join in," he said.

"No one cares what you look like—"

He pulled her closer, and eased the halter over her breasts, and kissed them. *The only man in the world who can have a naked woman in his bed, and lose her.*

"What *do* you want, Janet?"

She took his hand and rushed it to her cheek, which was moist with tears. "Paul—I beg you," she whispered, "I've never done it. It frightens me. Why does it have to be tonight?"

At that instant it occurred to him that the act of sex was insanely distant from both their needs; he had dreamt that evening only of an after-sex serenity. But something was driving him. His hand, an intruder, lay warm on her breast. "I was a virgin last year, too," he said. "It's a burden and nothing more."

"I want it to be as perfect as possible, whenever it happens. Every time, as perfect as possible. Tonight isn't right—tonight I really wanted to be like Ingrid, but look what happened when I tried . . ." Her sobs were audible for the first time. He stroked her hair until the crying passed. His thoughts drifted back to Boston, to the room of Anna the sculptress who shared his kitchen. During his first love-making, the odor of her cats had nearly sickened him.

"Janet—you're making me feel abnormal somehow for wanting you, even here, where they all assume we're lovers. But it's *you* who's making the demands. Is it so important to you that it has to be perfect? Who in his right mind takes sex as seriously as you?"

Her body softened. She lay quietly for several minutes. *Let me be your Olympic athlete, your Italian, and you be my stewardess, my Magnusdottir. . . .*

"You do," she said. "Only me and you do."

He dried her tears. "But not tonight," she said. "I couldn't control my body tonight. Please be patient with me a little longer." She kissed him, and crossed the room quickly to her bed. Out in the living room, he thought he heard a giggle—Ingrid's? Aino's?—a giggle that flattered him and brought a moment's peace.

"Paul?" Janet called. "That was a promise, O.K.?"

Sleep, when he finally surrendered, was brief and tiring. In the vault of the room—too black for resting, for even picking out the door and window—the old fears plagued him. Eternal perfection was all she wanted, *from him.* Perfection of a physical grace, from a man like Keeler who couldn't even dance. From out in the living room, came another soft and intimate giggle.

5

A cold light cut into the bedroom. Keeler listened for rain, and picked out its steady pattering on the window, the roof, and the glutted ground. His watch said six sharp. On a morning made for sleep, he was fully awake. On the other bed Janet slept, still and voluptuous, her midriff stippled with gooseflesh. Both her blankets had slipped to the floor. He swung out of bed, numbing his feet on the icy boards, and tucked her in. Then he dressed and through the window, took in the particulars of a dreary Swedish dawn.

He opened the bedroom door, at first a crack, fearful of disturbing the lovers on the living room floor. But they were facing one another, asleep and snoring. The room was warm. And as of course she would—*Es ist Schweden*—Ingrid slept nude, exposing her creamy back to Keeler at the moment. Aino lay swaddled on the sofa, her hair pooled like cold sunlight around her head. On the floor by a clogged ashtray, he spotted his manuscripts. He tiptoed through the living room, to the front door. The boards creaked, and Ingrid whimpered. Oh, no, he panicked—fearing detection and the unplotted voyeurism he'd have to explain—don't wake up, don't turn over. . . . He crept back to the bedroom and closed the door, just as Ingrid stretched with eyes still closed.

As he approached his bed, the anxiousness again engulfed him. His body needed action. Ignoring Janet, he raised the window and lifted himself over the sill for the short drop to the ground, nervous as a burglar. But the treasure slept on, and as he slithered down the sideboards, he wondered what kind of fool he was, shunning the bed for a frigid dawn.

He started jogging, easy enough for a flaccid writer, but joyously, his body demanded more. He gave it more, expecting a crippling pain which didn't come. The sodden path flew under his dancing sandals. Roots and rocks flattened to let him pass. Careening toward the ocean now, along an unpaved road, past empty cottages, he wondered what kind of German nut he'd be taken for—had he been seen—running and shouting "Valderee, Valdera . . ." in a late summer rain.

When the road petered into a sandy rut, Keeler, puffing, stormed the dunes like a training miler. From the final ledge, where the gray Baltic first rose into view, he leaped, and barely indented the rain-packed sand where he landed, a few feet below. There he collapsed, shivering. The sea spilled from the still-darkened West, and crashed in cold breakers nearly at his feet. It was a colorless scene: gray sky, black water, white sand, and a mist all over. He closed his eyes and let his dazed mind roam: in northern Europe, great cities were awakening to drizzle—hadn't he first seen Köln on such a day—and just a few miles East, across this island and a strait of choppy water, Russia stirred under a smudge of sun. And in Boston it's midnight, probably too hot for sleep . . . Paul Keeler, you are lost.

He strolled to the water's edge. It was *cold*. And noisy—such unattended noise was terrifying. A thousand bathers would go unheard. The beach was prime-vally desolate. A Viking longship could suddenly land. *Schweden.*

What the hell, he thought.

Facing the melted glacier of an ocean, he dropped his German trousers. Then the gritty jockey shorts. Then he slipped out of his clammy sweater and undershirt. Never, he mused, has there stood a more naked man. He tossed his socks and sandals on the pile of clothes, ran down the beach a few hundred yards gathering nerve, closed his eyes, then rushed the shrieking water. The first breaker cut him down into the sharpest pain he'd ever felt. One wave swept over him, then another; icy blankets that dropped him to his knees like a broken fighter. Bent double, he scrambled ashore before the next humiliation. His privates had wisely wizened and withdrawn. He dressed and jogged back to the cabin, soaked and out of breath, but still possessed by the idiot energy. Even so, he thought, if the day comes to nothing more, it's already been adventuresome. Shades of Ingmar Bergman; if only birch switches and a voracious woman were waiting.

By the time he reached the bedroom window, his legs were numb, and his side ached. He had painstakingly lifted one leg over the window sill to climb back in, when a girl's voice called from the front porch, "Are you there, Paul Keeler?" It was Aino. Before he could pull the leg back, she peered around the corner, her hair a mass of suds. "Whatever are you doing?"

". . . back inside . . ." he mumbled, struggling for breath.

"Come to the front. It is much easier that way, I believe." She disappeared. Keeler trudged to the porch.

Her back was to him, as she dipped low to a tub of water. The black sweater and bra were draped across the porch railing, where a cigarette smoldered. She jerked her head back, blowing spray in his direction. Then she turned and wrapped a towel around her body.

"It wouldn't do, you watching me like this, would it, Paul Keeler?"

"Not at all, Aino, not at all. Well, if you don't mind —" He climbed one step.

She sat on the top step and began drying her hair with vicious swipes of the giant towel. Keeler sat on the bottom step. He wanted desperately to get back inside. She blocked the steps. He began to shiver. "You've been swimming already."

"Just in and out, it was a crazy thing."

"So. You must prove things by yourself. But going in alone is no fun."

"I've got nothing against group sports, Aino."

"It is very popular in these countries. The King and the Queen do it, professors and students. One must learn not to be conscious of one's body, that's all."

"I'm sure that's all. But these things aren't easy for me. I wish they were."

"Janet liked it. She was disappointed you didn't come."

"And I was disappointed she went. I told her I'll go next time."

"When my hair is dry, Paul Keeler, then I go down to the beach. You come with me?"

"We'll see. I'm feeling a bit lightheaded at the moment."

"As you wish." She stood and dropped the towel as she stooped for her sweater. For an eternal moment she stood frozen before him—to turn away now would be the true embarrassment. He stared at the child-figure of Aino, who looked back with an ancient smile. Then she pulled her sweater on.

There is no childhood, Keeler thought, no innocence: the child-plumpness of her face, the globe-curve of her breasts, the trusting blue eyes and baby-fine hair—these are the marks of womanhood, never hardened, forever ready. This is no child. She sat down; Keeler moved up a step.

"Last night I stayed up and read your stories," she said. "Until the fire went out."

He laughed, thinking of the long nights spent writing them in Boston, in the kitchen warmed by an oven. "That's how they should be read."

"You are very good, I think. I do not know many American writers, but you are like a Russian named Chekhov, a little. You know Russian?"

"No."

"You know him, perhaps? He is very popular in Finland."

"He'll do, Aino. But how, exactly, am I like him?"

"He writes of humiliation. You Americans cannot do that, because you are not humble. But I think you are, a little. Your stories are, a little. You can make people live. I envy that, Paul Keeler. Next year I become just a dietician in the north of Finland."

"What a thing, Aino." He bowed his head and stared at the pools of black water collecting under the steps. *I know a dietician in the north of Finland . . .*

"Paul Keeler, I would like you to make love to me."

The little pools drew suddenly close, reflecting like tiny eyes. He looked up. She was folding the towel, staring at him with head cocked sideways.

"I can't. I couldn't, Aino, I'm here with Janet. Maybe things are different here, but not that different for us—" None of it sounded convincing, even though he believed it.

"I am not talking about how it is for Swedes, or for Americans, Paul Keeler," she cut in with a frown. "Anyway, I have asked Janet and I know you are not sleeping together. You hold her breast."

Oh God, he thought, and dropped his head.

"And I have asked if she minded us doing it," Aino finished triumphantly.

"And she agreed?"

"She said it was up to you." Aino opened the screen door and turned. "My coffee is ready," she said in a low voice. "I take some, then go for my swim. Come with me or stay if you wish." She caught the door before it slammed.

His ears were burning, his face glowed with shame. Is Janet testing me? Take Aino and I'm a cad, refuse her and I'm half a man. How would *I* react if Bengt came to me and put his intentions so innocently? Half ashamed, he could see himself assenting, trusting Janet's fears, or scruples, to save him from mortification.

Aino brought him coffee, and sat a step above him as

they drank. "It is Ingrid's cup, I hope you don't mind," she explained. The marvelous coffee stretched his nerves afresh and reflected his face, oblong and flat, on its surface. He watched himself for a while, a stranger. This new hesitation was not the old one of Place Pigalle; in the crevices of his pants he was coming alive.

Nothing he had done in the past two years had brought him comfort. Self-denial in Boston had made him a fool. He'd come to Europe for the oldest reasons—love and culture—and still he felt lost. He had a vision, a remote one, that the man he wanted to be was forty years old with a thousand beautiful women in his past. A kind, considerate, forty-year-old artist who could sit for hours on the Champs Élysées, ignoring the woman of his dreams for the simple reason that he no longer dreamed.

He glanced at Aino, who smiled back, again the child, short and plump, with wet spires of blond hair bristling from her head. She lit a cigarette.

"I have finished the coffee, Paul Keeler."

"I'm still drinking, Aino. Hold on a while."

"I will wash my cup. Then I go for my swim." She went inside, and Keeler followed her, whispering as he passed, "I'll be a few minutes, at least." An instinct possessed him—to see Janet. Maybe just to see her.

Bengt and Ingrid were still asleep, unmoved from their position of an hour before. The bedroom door was open and Janet was awake, propped on a pillow with her suitcase open at her feet. She was pale, her nose red, her hair damp and matted, fighting the comb with every swipe. The room reminded Keeler of a hospital, and in the harsh light Janet seemed a stranger, bitter and lonely.

"I didn't want to wake you." He sat on her bed and placed his hands over her blanketed feet.

"Aino woke me up," she said. Her voice was husky. A cold was coming on, and she had been crying. "It seems she liked your stories very much."

"I've already talked to her. Janet, why did you tell her *everything*? I just talked to her outside, and *why*—how could you do that to me?"

"Do what?"

"Make it public. That I . . . that we . . . that I'm holding your breast, as Aino put it."

She brought her knees up high and propped her forehead between them. "I truly didn't think the truth would embarrass you. But I can't go swimming naked with people and then lie to them. It was the most natural answer in the world, and when she asked me it was the only answer I could give." She looked over her knees, her eyes clear and dry, and sad.

"It was the most natural question in the world, too," said Keeler. "She's asked me to make love to her. Does that surprise you?"

Her glance was steady, riveted somewhere behind his head. Then she shook her head. "No, I'm not surprised. Mad, a little. I didn't think she was so . . . hard up, I guess, to take someone else's friend."

"She's *not* hard up—she doesn't care! That's what's different about her."

"Do you find her attractive?"

"Now I do, yes. What difference does it make? You're

forcing me to live with illusions, Janet, then you shatter them. I can't take that."

"What illusions?"

"That we're lovers. That any hour now this tension will just end. Magically. I'm sorry, but I can't live with that."

"Or the truth?"

"Especially the truth." He stood, and backed to the door. Janet drew the covers close and eased herself against the wall.

"So. You're going to her?"

"I don't know."

Bengt coughed, and called, "*Guten Morgen!*" Keeler slammed the door for privacy. "Janet—let's go away from here. We can leave today and still have a month together. We'll go someplace else where it's a little less perfect. It's too open here, we can't handle it. People like Aino will be asking questions, and you'll be telling the truth, and I'll be telling lies—we're not ready for it yet. It's our only chance."

"Where do you have in mind?"

"I don't know. Norway, maybe. Denmark. Germany. I don't care. Yes, I do—somewhere I speak the language. England. France. I'm just not ready for someone to call '*Guten Morgen*' when I think I'm alone. Last night it's nude swimming, this morning it's a proposition—it's stimulating, but it's too much."

"These are my friends, and I've worked for this. I don't care to be a tourist, thank you. What I've gone through this year you'll never know. I'm not leaving."

"Then I am." He eased the door open.

She rolled out of bed. "Close the door," she said. Keeler leaned against it. "Don't go. I'm ready." She stood before the window, clutching her elbows for warmth, but not advancing. She curled her fingers under the halter, turned her back, then slowly lifted the halter, peeling it over her head, and dropping it on the bed.

"How's this?" She turned. He forgot about her face, her mussed hair, and concentrated on her flesh, full and white, nervous. "Stay . . . stay," she pleaded, as her fingers found the elastic of the panties and began rolling them down, down, till they too fell on the floor and she was standing before him nude, biting her lip. He took a step toward her and she leaped into bed, pulling the covers around her neck.

"Now you can have me—here," she cried, "right now. Right now," her voice much louder than she perhaps intended. He rushed to quiet her, and she squirmed farther into the corner, pulling her knees even higher. Her eyes were closed, and her face was set in readiness for pain when Keeler took her hand.

"Janet—"

"Are you going to rape me?" Her eyes opened wide, terror-struck, as she cried again, louder, "Are you going to rape me?"

He seized her hands and forced them to her knees. The blanket dropped and for a moment they stared at each other, over her full, open bosom. She began crying, softly, then more loudly as she struggled to catch her breath.

"Quiet down." As he sat there, restraining her hands, he realized that there was nothing he'd rather do *now* than rape her. Then he laughed. If this were the movies, he would slap her and she would embrace him, sensibly and passionately, begging his forgiveness. He dropped her hands, covered her, then left her, nude and crying, bundled in the corner of her bed.

Bengt was awake, propped on an elbow, when Keeler opened the door. "*Guten Morgen*," he greeted, as Keeler dashed across the living room to the front door. Aino had gone. He set out after her, down the path to the sea, under the dripping boughs. He came to the dunes a few hundred feet past the bunker, doubled back along the crumbling ridge, and collapsed finally at the bunker's face in the pocked and hardened sand, by the pile of Aino's clothes. Just below him she was bathing; a white pillar in the somber water. Her cries, high and excited, carried over the surf, borne by the wind that whistled from the mainland. He spread her clothes in a kind of blanket on the leeward slope of sand, waved, and waited. The sea had turned warm for her.

The sun was brighter, a sharp headlamp cutting the clouds behind him. He thought of himself as he'd been in Luxembourg, riding the train to Köln. Himself in Pigalle. He could do it now, be a Phi Gam if he wanted. He unbuttoned his trousers. There was nothing to it, really. He faced the path, hoping to see Janet running his way, but it tunneled into the trees, dark and quiet. He pulled off his sweater and turned again to face the sea.

The Thibidault

Stories

Indeed it is not unusual for the memory to
condense into a single mythic moment the
contingencies and perpetual rebeginnings
of an individual human history.

Sartre

Saint Genet

The Bridge

1

Studio One *reached Fort Lauderdale from* the Dumont station in Miami, and in the summer I was allowed up late enough to watch it. We had no set at home, having recently come down from Montreal. I watched it at Rifkin Brothers Furniture and Appliance Center, where my father was the furniture buyer. The sets were round with magnifying lenses bracketed in front. The hostess of *Studio One* was Betty Furness, the Westinghouse lady.

An enormous sense of power, watching television behind locked doors while people press their faces to the windows—a seven-year-old responds to that. Behind me in the dark, mannequins in evening dresses stood by their washing machines, and upstairs my father worked on the books.

Around seven o'clock his secretary would come down from the office and sit with me in front of the television, and talk. She had a northern voice, and a harsh one, but no demands were in it. I knew (in the way of a boss's son) that she liked me. I knew, in fact, she thought I was amazing. She took me out to get the coffee and sandwiches, a high-point of the evening. A child hungers for that. There's something illicit in going out with a pretty secretary for coffee and sandwiches.

Joan was her name. She'd been introduced to me as Joan and a boss's son has that privilege, even when he is fast becoming a *yes ma'am-no ma'am* southern boy and is otherwise overly polite. I called her Joan because I never learned her last name. Born a Larivière up in New Hampshire (where they pronounced it "Larry Veer"), she had been divorced from a Georgian named Holman after being widowed in the war by a man named Paulson. Widowed at eighteen and divorced on the rebound, and still only twenty-five. She was tiny but ample, and depending on the day and what she wore, became a trifle plump or unbearably voluptuous. The word, I know now, was *ripe*. Her arms were full and downy, her waistline faultless but a little too sudden, no room for a curving back and leisurely midriff, the gentle reach and suppression of breasts and hips, and I, at seven, responded to that. She was old enough to be my sister, but *just* to be my sister, and that accounted for the whistles she got on the way to the carryout counter at the big Walgreen's a block away.

With the television on and my father in the back behind the door, I would prowl the darkened store, trying chairs and sofas, and far from the windows where people could watch me, I dug my well-scrubbed hands into the mannequins' dresses, over their cold unnippled breasts and up their fused and icy thighs. All of the mannequins immobile, unprotesting, Betty Furnesses. By the middle of the evening, I'd have all the girls

unbuttoned, then by ten o'clock, have them proper once
again.

2

We Thibidaults went to the beach one weekday, a day
of perfect calm. My parents lay on a blanket sleeping
and I ventured out. I couldn't swim. The Atlantic was
glassy, even calmer than the Gulf but without the slime
of jellyfish. Just the weeds with spotted crabs. I walked
out in the perfect neutral warmth, in piss-warm water,
not flinching with the darts of minnows against my legs,
not worried about sand sharks and manta rays, barracuda
beyond the jetties. I'd read of the fishes, knew the
dangers, but still I walked. No waves in sight, the convoy
of giant tankers steamed across the horizon, and the
illusion was firm that I could walk that day to Dakar or
Lisbon. I bounced to shoulder-depth, knowing that if I
stumbled or if something large should strike my legs,
if a wave or undertow should suddenly arise, I would
drown. At chin-depth I tried to turn and couldn't without taking another half-step forward to gain my balance.
I opened my mouth to call, but only whimpered, and
water entered. I thought I saw the dark funneling
shapes of my worst nightmares, and my throat closed
with fear. I tried to walk backward and stumbled.
My head went under, water invaded my ears, and then
I was lifted, carried back a step or two, and set down
in shoulder-depth water. My chest was still locked and
my father struck me, hard, as he turned. I coughed as

I ran behind him, afraid to look back. *"Dites rien à Maman,"* he said, and joined my mother who had not wakened. He never spoke of it to me, or to her.

3

Fort Lauderdale had a city pool, a Spanish-style fortress across from the beach. Swimming lessons were free in fresh, icy water under a murderous summer sun. We lived four miles from the ocean on a brackish, unswimmable estuary called the Tarpon River. The river swarmed with eels, crabs, mullet, and catfish, and I had caught and studied them all, and lost yards of line and dozens of hooks to the garbage fish that gasped and bubbled under our dock. But such is access to the ocean; before you charter a boat you haul up eels; before skindiving you learn to paddle. And you learn the ocean in the Municipal Pool.

I never learned. The water stunned me with its iciness. It was a July day in the upper nineties. The noontime sun was a lamp that bleached the skies and burned through the droplets of water on my back. I tried to float and felt torn by the scalding sun on my back and the numbing cold that gripped my legs and belly. I wanted to sink into the dancing blueness, the cold Canadianness of the water. No one watched, and bronzed Florida kids played dangerous games in the deep end. I left.

I had biked out barefoot, towel around my shoulders, feeling very Floridian and almost at home. It was four miles from our house to the pool, down Las Olas Boulevard. A scorching day. Las Olas was intersected by an old swing bridge over the Inland Waterway which I, returning from the pool, towel on the handle bars drying, now approached. The bridge was out to let a string of yachts pass under. It wasn't returning in time to allow the backed-up cars to start and finally my bicycle began to wobble. I put my bare foot down to steady it and suddenly I screamed. The black-top was gummy from the sun, my foot already tar-stained and burning. The bicycle toppled, spilling the towel on the crushed limestone shoulder. The wooden bridge was now back in place and the guardrail was lifting, but I was crouched in the burning limestone. My bike and towel had rolled several feet behind me. The stones gave way to a sheer drop to the waterway about fifty feet below; my only hope was in dashing to the bridge, a splintery weathered thing, itself hot, but equipped with a rail that I could lean over until my feet quit burning. And then my bike was farther away than ever and walking to it barefoot over the burning limestone or over the soggy black-top seemed almost Fijian, something natives did in the *National Geographic*. My eyes watered in the blank sunlight. I looked at my arms and shoulders and they were as white as a slice of baker's bread.

Cars whizzed past, glittering in the sun, their windshields, hoods, and chromework so bright that I couldn't face them. Everywhere I looked there was a haze of pink. It was like coming out of a Saturday matinee after three hours in the dark and letting the white buildings blind you. No one was out walking, not at noontime over the unshaded bridge with just a bait and tackle shop at the far end. No one ever walked in the States, my mother had said.

The door of the bait shop opened. Way in the distance an old man started my way, drinking a bottle of orange and carrying a white carton of live bait-shrimp. He was still talking to the owner as he walked away, and finally he laughed loudly and waved. I could taste the orange-ade prickling my mouth as the man shambled toward me. An old man, dressed warmly on a blistering day, took a final swig leaving an inch or so on the bottom, and flung the bottle over the railing and into the Water-way.

"Sir!" I called, long before the man could hear. My voice was weak against the traffic and seemed to be whining, like the voices of tourist kids in restaurants.

"Sir!"

The man drew near, holding the shrimp by a frail wire loop. The shrimp smelled, the water sloshed. I knew I could drink it.

"Sir—would you get my bike for me, please?"

The man walked past, smiling at his shrimp, squinting against the oncoming cars. "Sir—please, please. My feet are burnt and I can't walk—" but my voice was coming out a whimper and he didn't turn around. He just crunched on over the limestone in his thick oily boots and was past my bike without looking down. Then he faded and I had to blink to keep him in sight. He climbed down the bank and settled by the water to fish.

I lowered myself to the wooden planks. My shadow had made the wood bearable for my knees, then my legs, and finally I curled myself on the wood against the railings. There was a tiny knothole by my toes and I bent over, until my back seemed ready to split, like a roasted pig's I'd once seen in the *National Geographic*. The limestone looked like white-hot coals.

Through the knothole the water seemed even closer, like Coke at the bottom of a bottle. If I'd had a straw, I could suck it through, and I remembered the day I almost drowned, when ocean water hadn't tasted all that bad. Now, blue, running and deep, it seemed a cool blanket to wrap my shoulders in.

And when the water became olive-dark, strange shapes began to flutter; the channel seemed opaque, then shallow. I clung to the railing now, so large did the knothole seem; so close did the lapping of water against the pilings sound. The channel bottom was heaving and rolling; bubbles rose, currents dimpled, needlefish glided on the surface, mullet teemed around the pilings, snook leaped, a cabin cruiser that didn't need the bridge to turn, gurgled under me, shattering the water for several minutes, the old people on board drinking beer from ice chests, maybe trawling, and playing cards. I thought of taking down my swimsuit and pissing through the knothole on the next boat that passed. Maybe if I took off my pants and stood naked on the bridge someone would stop and give me water; but I was afraid of getting in trouble. I lifted my head a minute and stared at the highway, now vague and white. I had the impression that I was going to die and that dying on the bridge with hundreds of cars passing would be more pathetic than anything. People would know how I had felt. The old man fishing on the bank would be caught and thrown in jail. The bait man at the end of the bridge and the bridge man who must have been watching for the past two or three hours from his little perch at the far end, and the people on the boats who had passed underneath and all the cars that had hissed past on a film of melted asphalt; all guilty of letting me die. If I'd wanted to talk now I couldn't, my mouth was as dry as my back, and my tongue had grown to my palate. The water under the bridge was olive now and my gaze penetrated far below the surface. The wooden railing jiggled slightly. I held on, afraid that I might tip head-first through the peephole. I couldn't feel my body against the wood; it was as though I were asleep in bed with my head sinking into the cool pillow and my feet rising slowly. In the water, which now seemed shallow, something enormous, flat and brown, tipped a wing and then settled back. The surface shuddered in response.

"I think—" A voice that seemed to be coming from the wood of the bridge, and I had to force myself to remember that I was just a foot or two from the highway, and in the middle of a sidewalk. I tried to look up to see who it was, for the voice was familiar, but, as in a dream, I couldn't. I felt now as though my feet were waving high and I was somehow balancing on the sharpened pupil of my eye. But when a hand came down on my back, I twitched, banging my nose.

"My God, the skin—look at his back! I told you that was his bike, didn't I? Go down to that bait shop and bring me some water. He's unconscious."

My father.

I couldn't waken to speak. His hands were under me now, trying to lift me in my bent position, but any movement was like palming hot sand over broken blisters, and the moment I was lifted from the knothole, the instant water was removed and everything again turned white and wooden, I began to shiver, then to retch. I wanted only to be dropped in cool water and allowed to sleep. I opened one eye, just enough for light to enter, and saw the waterway, and on the surface, as though I had conjured them at last, a school of manta rays, skimming the surface and slapping their way out of sight. Then I slept, hearing voices and my father's response, "I'm taking him home, yes, I'm his father, yes, I've been searching all over . . ."

When I wakened it was shady, in a car, in the arms —I could tell even with my eyes closed—of a young woman who had recently showered. The doors of the car were open, I could feel a warm breeze, though I shivered, and the ashtrays had not been cleaned.

"It's frightening," she said. "How close—"

My back was cooler but the pain was deep, more like cuts than a burn. I would have vomited but felt too weak. "I mean if we hadn't of . . . You'd better take him now," she said, "he feels a little cooler." The doors slammed and my father said, "I'll let you off first," I fluttered my eyes but couldn't keep them open. "All right," she said, and I could feel her looking down at me, stroking my hair, "Such a little boy, really," and then, "It would be bad if he saw me here," she said in that harsh Yankee voice. And before I slept she added in that soft Canadian French of her childhood, and mine, "*Mal si'l me voit.*"

[141]

The Salesman's Son Grows Older

Camphor berries popped underfoot on a night as hot and close as a faucet of sweat. My mother and I were walking from the movies. It was late for me but since my father was on the road selling furniture, she had taken me out. She watched the sidewalk for roaches darting to the gutters. They popped like berries underfoot. I was sleepy and my mother restless, like women whose men are often gone. She hadn't eaten supper, hadn't read the paper, couldn't stand the radio, and finally she'd suggested the movies. Inside, she'd paced behind the glass while I watched a Margaret O'Brien movie. The theater was air-cooled, which meant the hot air was kept circulating; even so the outdoors had been formidable under a moon that burned hotly. The apartment would be crushing. She'd been a week without a letter.

I think now of the privileges of the salesman's son, as much as the moving from town to town, the post cards and long-distance calls; staying up late, keeping my mother company, being her confidant, behaving even at eight a good ten years older. And always wondering with her where my father was. Somewhere in his territory, anywhere from Raleigh to Shreveport. Another privilege of the salesman's son was knowing the cities and the routes between them, knowing the miles and predicting how long any drive would take. As a child, I'd wanted to be a Greyhound driver.

The smell of a summer night in Florida is so strong that twenty years later on a snowy night in Canada I can still feel it. Lustrous tropical nights, full of roaches and rats and lizards, with lightning bugs and whip-poor-wills pricking the dark and silence. I wanted to walk past our apartment house to the crater of peat bogs just beyond, so that the sweat on my arms could at least evaporate.

"Maybe daddy'll be home tonight," I said, playing the game of the salesman's son. There was a cream-colored sedan in our driveway, with a white top that made it look like my father's convertible. Then the light went on inside and the door opened and a drowsy young patrolman with his tie loosened and his Stetson and clipboard shuffled our way.

"Ma'am, are you the party in the upper apartment? I mean are you Mrs. Thee . . . is this here your name, ma'am?"

"Thibidault," she said. "*T. B. Doe* if you wish."

"I wonder then can we go inside a spell?"

"What is it?"

"Let's just go inside so's we can set a spell."

A long climb up the back staircase, my mother breathing deeply, long *ah-h-h's* and I took the key from her to let us in. I threw open the windows and turned on the lights. The patrolman tried to have my mother sit. She knew what was coming, like a miner's wife at a sudden whistle. She went to the kitchen and opened a Coke for me and poured iced tea for the young patrolman, then came back and sat where he told her to.

"You're here to tell me my husband is dead. I've felt it all night." Her head was nodding, a way of commanding agreement. "I'll be all right."

She wouldn't be, I knew. She'd need me.

"I didn't say that, ma'am," and for the first time his eyes brightened. "No, ma'am, he isn't dead. There was a pretty bad smash-up up in Georgia about three days ago and he was unconscious till this morning. The report we got is he was on the critical list but they done took him off. He's in serious condition."

"How serious is serious?" I asked.

"What?"

She was still nodding. "You needn't worry. You can go if you wish—you've been very considerate."

"Can I fetch you something? Is there anybody you want me to call? Lots of times the effect of distressing news don't sink in till later and it's kindly useful having somebody around."

"Where did you say he was?"

He rustled the papers on his clipboard, happy to oblige. "Georgia, ma'am, Valdosta—that's about two hundred mile north. This here isn't the official report but it says the accident happened about midnight last Wednesday smack in the middle of Valdosta. Mr. Thee

. . . Mr. *Doe,* was alone in the car and they reckon he must have fell asleep. The car . . . well, there ain't much left of the car."

"Did he hurt anyone else?"

"No, ma'am. Least it don't say so here." He grinned. "Looks like it was just him."

She was angry.

"Why wasn't I notified earlier?" she asked.

"That's kindly irregular ma'am. I don't know why."

She nodded. She hadn't stopped nodding.

"We can call up to Valdosta and get you a place to stay. And we'll keep an eye on this place while you're gone. *Anything you want,* Mrs. Doe, that's what I'm aimin' to say."

She was silent for a long time as though she were going to say, *Would you repeat it please, I don't think I heard it right:* and there was even a smile on her face, not a happy one, a smile that says *life is long and many things happen that we can't control and can't change and can't bring back.* "You've been very helpful. Please go."

If my father were dead it meant we would move. Back to Canada perhaps. Or west to the mountains, north to cities. And if my father lived, that too would change our lives, somehow. My mother stayed in the living room after the officer left and I watched her from the crack of my door, drinking hot coffee and smoking more than she ever had before. A few minutes later came a knock on the front door and she hurried to open up. Two neighbor women whose children I knew but rarely played with stepped inside and poured themselves iced tea, then waited to learn what had brought the police to the Yankee lady's door.

My mother said there'd been an accident.

"I knowed it was that," said Mrs. Wade, "and him such a fine-looking gentleman, too. I seen the po-lice settin' in your drive all evenin'-long and I said to my Grady that poor woman and her li'l boy is in for bad news when they get back from the pitchershow—or wherever you was at—so I called Miz Davis here and told her what I seen and wouldn't you know she said we best fix up a li'l basket of fruit—that's kindly like a custom with us here, since I knowed you was from outastate. What I brung ain't much just some navels and tangerines but I reckon it's somethin' to suck on when the times is bad."

"I reckon," said Mrs. Davis, "your mister was hurt pretty bad."

"Yes."

"They told you where he's at, I reckon."

"Yes, they did."

"Miz Davis and me, we thought if you was going to see him you'd need somebody to look after your li'l boy. I don't want you to go on worryin' your head over that at all. Her and her Billy got all the room he's fixin' to need."

"That's very kind."

I was out of bed now and back at the crack of my opened door. I'd never seen my mother talk to any neighbor women. I'd never been more aware of how different she looked and sounded. And of all the exciting possibilities opened up by my father's accident and possible death, staying back in an unpainted shanty full of loud kids was the least attractive. I began wishing my father wasn't hurt. And then I realized that the neighbor women with their sympathy and fruit had broken my mother's resistance. She would cry as soon as they left and I would have to pretend to be asleep, or else go out and comfort her, bring her tea and listen to her; be a salesman's son.

Audrey Davis was plump and straight-haired; Billy was gaunt, red-cheeked, and almost handsome. The children came in a phalanx of older girls who'd already run off, then a second wave ranging from the nearly pubescent down to infancy. At eight, I fell in the middle of the second pack whose leader was a ten-year-old named Carrie, with ear-rings and painted nails.

They ate their meals fried or boiled. Twenty years later I can still taste their warm, sweet tea, the fat chunks of pork, the chick peas, and okra. I can still smell the outhouse and hear the hiss of a million maggots flashing silver down the hole. The Davis crap was the fairest yellow. The food? Disease?

But what I really remember, and remember with such vividness that even now I wince, is this: sleeping one night on the living room rug—it was red and worn down to its backing—I developed a cough. After some rustling in the back Miz Davis appeared at the door, clad in a robe tied once at the waist. One white tubular breast had worked free. The nipple was poised like an ornament at its tip. It was the first time I'd ever seen a breast.

Even as I was watching it, she set to work with a mixture for the cough. By the time I noticed the liquid and the spoon, she was adding sugar. I opened wide, anxious to impress, and she thrust in the spoon, far enough to make me gag, and pulled my head back by the hair. She kept the spoon inside until I felt I was drowning in the gritty mixture of sugar and kerosene. I knew if I was dying there was one thing I wanted to do; I brought my open hand against the palm-numbing softness of her breast, then, for an instant ran my fingertips over the hard, dry nipple and shafts of prickly hair. She acted as though nothing had happened and I looked innocent as though nothing had been intended. Then she took out the spoon.

After Audrey Davis's breast and kerosene my excreta turned a runny yellow. The night after the breast I was hiding in the sawgrass, bitten by mosquitoes and betrayed by fireflies, playing kick-the-can. The bladder-burning tension was excrutiating for a slow, chubby boy in a running game, scurrying under the Davis jeep, under the pilings of the house, into the edges of the peat. My breath, cupped in the palm of my sweating hand, echoed like a deep-sea diver's as Carrie Davis beat the brush looking for me. Chigger bites, mosquito welts, burned and itched. I wanted to scream, to lift the house on my shoulders, to send the can in a spiraling arch sixty yards downfield, splitting imaginary goal posts and freeing Carrie's prisoners but I knew—knew—that even if I snuck away undetected, even with a ten-foot lead on Carrie or anyone else, I'd lose the dash to the can. Even if I got there first I'd kick too early and catch it with my glancing heel and the can would lean and roll and be replaced before I could hide again. I knew finally that it would be my fate, if caught, to be searching for kids in a twenty-foot circle for the rest of the night, or until the Davis kids got tired of running and kicking the can from under me. Better, then, to huddle deep in the pilings, deeper even than the hounds would venture till I could smell the muck, the seepage from the outhouse, the undried spillage from the kitchen slops. No one would find me. I wouldn't be caught nor would I ever kick the goddam can. Time after time, game after game, after the kids were caught they'd have to call, "Frankie, Frankie, come in free," and it would be exasperation, not admiration, that tinted Carrie's voice.

My mother came back four days later and set about selling all the clothes and furniture that anyone wanted. There were brief discussions with the neighbor women who shook their heads as she spoke. Finally I drew the conclusion that my father was dead, though I didn't ask. I tried out this new profound distinction on Carrie Davis and was treated for a day or two with a deference, a near sympathy ("Don't you do that, Billy Joe, can't you see his daddy's dead?") that I'd been seeking all along and probably ever since.

But how was it, in the week or so that it took her to pack and sell off everything that I never asked her what exactly had happened in Valdosta? Her mood had been grim and businesslike, the mood a salesman's son learns not to tamper with. I adjusted instead to the news that we were leaving Florida and would be returning to her family in Saskatchewan.

Saskatchewan! No neighbor had ever heard of it. "Where in the world's that at?" my teacher asked when I requested the transfer slip. When I said Canada, she asked what state. The Davis kids had never heard of Canada.

One book that had always traveled with us was my mother's Atlas. She had used it in school before the Great War—a phrase she still used—a comprehensive British edition that smeared the world in Imperial reds and pinks so that my vision of the earth had been distorted by Edwardian lenses. Safe pink swaths cut the rift of Africa, the belly of Asia, and lighted like a rash over Oceania and the Caribbean. And of course red dominated and overwhelmed poor North America. The raw, pink, bulging brow of the continent was Canada, the largest and reddest blob of Britishness in the flat projection of the world. Saskatchewan alone could hold half a dozen Texases and the undivided yellow of the desert southwest called the "Indian Territories."

It was the smell of the book that had attracted me and led me, even before I could read, to a tracing of the Ottoman Empire, Austro-Hungary, and a dozen princely states. That had been my mother's childhood world and it became mine too—cool, confident, and British—and now it seems to me, that all the disruptions in my life and in Mildred Blankenship's have merely been a settling of the old borders, an insurrection of the cool gazetteer with its sultanates, Boer lands, Pondichérys, and Port Arthurs. All in the frontispiece, with

its two-toned map of the world in red and gray em-
blazoned, *WE HOLD A GREATER EMPIRE THAN
HAS BEEN.*

We rode for a week without a break. Too excited for
sleep, I crouched against the railings behind the driver's
seat with a road map in my hand, crossing off towns and
county lines, then the borders of states. We'd left in
April; we were closing in on winter again. The drivers
urged me to talk, so they wouldn't fall asleep. "Watch
for a burnt-out gas station over the next rise," they'd
say, "three men got killed there . . . Down there a new
Stucky's is going up . . . Right at that guardrail is where
eight people got killed in a head-on crash . . ." And on
and on, identifying every town before it came, pacing
themselves like milers, "Must be 3:15," they'd say, passing an all-night diner and tooting a horn, knowing every
night clerk in every small-town hotel where the bundles
of morning papers were thrown off. It had seemed
miraculous, then, to master a five-state route as though
it were an elevator ride in a three-story department store.
Chattanooga to Indianapolis, four times a week. And
on we went: Chicago, Rock Island, Ottumwa, Des
Moines, Omaha, Sioux Falls, Pierre, and Butte, where
my uncle John Blankenship was on hand to take us
into Canada.

I watched my uncle for signs of foreignness. His
clothes were shaggy, the car was English, and there were
British flags in the corners of the windshield. But he
looked like a fleshed-out Billy Davis from Oshacola
County, Florida, with the same scraped cheeks, high

coloring and sky-blue eyes, the reddened hands with flaking knuckles, stubby fingers with stiff black hair. John's accent was as strange as the Davises'. The voice was deep, the patterns rapid, and each word emerged as hard and clear as cubes from a freezer.

The border town had broad dirt streets. A few of the cars parked along the elevated sidewalks were high, boxy, prewar models I couldn't identify. The cigarette signs, the first thing a boy notices, were foreign.

"How does it feel, Franklin? The air any different?"

"It might be, sir."

"You don't have to say 'sir' to me. Uncle John will do. You're in your own country now—just look at the land, will you? Look at the grain elevators—that's where our money is, in the land. Don't look for it in that chrome-plated junk. You can *see* the soil, can't you?"

The land was flat, about like Florida, the road straight and narrow and the next town's grain elevator already visible. It was late April and the snow had receded from the road-bed. Bald spots, black and glistening, were appearing in the fields under a cold bright sun. Three weeks ago, when my father was alive, the thermometer had hit ninety-five degrees.

"Of course you can. Grade A Saskatchewan hard, the finest in the world."

The finest what? I wondered.

"Far as the eye can see. That's prosperity, Mildred. And we haven't touched anything yet—we're going to be a rich province, Mildred. We have the largest potash reserves in the world. You'll have no trouble getting work, believe me."

"And how's Valerie?" my mother asked. "And the children?"

Around such questions I slowly unwound. My uncle was no bus driver and Saskatchewan offered nothing for a map-primed child. I was a British subject with a Deep South accent, riding in a cold car with a strong new uncle. So many new things to be ashamed of—my accent, my tan, my chubbiness. I spoke half as fast as my uncle and couldn't speed up.

"Ever been to a bonspiel, Franklin?"

"No, sir, I don't think so."

"You'll come out tonight, then. Your Aunt Valerie is skip."

I decided not to say another word. Not until I understood what the Canadians were talking about.

Uncle John Blankenship, that tedious man, and his wife and three children made room for us in Saskatoon. A cold spring gave way, in May, to a dry, burning heat, the kind that blazed across my forehead and shrunk the skin under my eyes and over my nose. But I didn't sweat. It wasn't like Florida heat that reached up groggily from the ground as well as from above, steaming the trouser cuffs while threatening sun stroke. The Blankenships had a farm out of town and Jack, my oldest cousin, ran a trap line and kept a .22 rifle in the loft of the barn. During the summer I spent hot afternoons firing at gophers as they popped from their holes. Fat boy with a gun, squinting over the wheat through July and August, the combine harvesting the beaten rows, months after believing my father dead, and happy. As happy as I've ever been.

I looked for help from my cousins, for cousins are the unborn brothers and sisters of the only child. But they were slightly older, more capable, and spoke strangely. They were never alone, never drank Cokes which were bad for the teeth and stomach (demonstrated for me by leaving a piece of metal in a cup of Coke), never seemed to tire of work and fellowship. They were up at five, worked hard till seven, ate hot meaty-mushy breakfasts, then raced back to work and came to lunch red in the brow, basted in sweat, yet not smelling bad at all. They drank pasteurized milk with flecks of cream and even when they rested in the early afternoon they'd sit outside with a motor in their lap and a kerosene-soaked rag to clean it. I would join them, but with an ancient issue of *Collier's* or *National Geographic* taken from the pillars of bundled magazines in the attic, and all afternoon I'd sit in the shade with my busy cousins, reading about "New Hope for Ancient Anatolia" or "Brave Finland Carries On." I was given an article from an old *Maclean's* about my grandfather, Morley Blankenship, a wheat pool president who had petitioned thirty thankless years for left-hand driving in Canada.

What about those cousins who'd never ceased working, who'd held night jobs through college, then married and gone to law school or whatever? *My* cousins, *my* unborn brothers with full Blankenship and McLeod blood and their medical or legal practices in Vancouver and Regina and their spiky, balding blond heads and their political organizing. Is that all their work and muscles and fresh air could bring them? Is that what I would have been if we'd stayed in Saskatoon, a bloody Blankenship with crinkles and crow's-feet at twenty-five?

And what if we'd stayed anywhere? If we'd never left Montreal, I'd have been educated in both my languages instead of Florida English. Or if we'd never left the South I'd have emerged a man of breeding, liberal in the traditions of Duke University with tastes for Augustan authors and breeding falcons, for quoting de Tocqueville and Henry James, a wearer of three-piece suits, a user of straight razors. What calamity made me a reader of back issues, defunct Atlases, and foreign grammars? The loss, the loss! To leave Montreal for places like Georgia and Florida; to leave Florida for Saskatchewan; to leave the prairies for places like Cincinnati and Pittsburgh and, finally, to stumble back to Montreal a middle-class American from a broken home, after years of pointless suffering had promised so much.

My son sleeps so soundly. Over his bed, five license plates are hung, the last four from Quebec, the first from Wisconsin. Five years ago, when he was six months old, we left to take a bad job in Montreal, where I was born but had never visited. My parents had brought me to the U.S. when I was six months old. Canada was at war, America was neutral. America meant opportunity, freedom; Montreal meant ghettos, and insults. And so, loving our children, we murder them. Following the sun, the dollars, the peace-of-mind, we blind ourselves. Better to be a professor's son than a salesman's son—better a thousand times, I think—better to ski than to feed the mordant hounds, better to swim at a summer cottage than debase yourself in the septic mud. But what do these license plates mean? Endurance? Exile, cunning? Where will we all wind up, and how?

Because I couldn't master the five-cent nib that all the Saskatoon kids had to use in school, and because the teacher wouldn't accept my very neat Florida pencil writing, a compromise was reached that allowed me to write in ball-point. I was now a third-grader.

The fanciest ball-point pen on sale in Saskatoon featured the head and enormous black hat of Hopalong Cassidy. The face was baby-pink with blue spots for eyes and white ones for teeth and sideburns. It was, naturally, an unbalanced thing that hemorrhaged purpley on the page. The ink was viscous and slow-drying and tended to accumulate in the cross-roads of every loop. Nevertheless, it was a handsome pen and the envy of my classmates, all of whom scratched their way Scottishly across the page.

One day in early October I had been sucking lightly on Hoppy's hat as I thought of the sum I was trying to add. I didn't know, but my mouth was purpling with a stream of ink and the blue saliva was trickling on my shirt. My fingers had carried it to my cheeks and eyes, over my forehead and up my nostrils. I noticed nothing. But suddenly the teacher gasped and started running toward me, and two students leaped from their desk to grab me.

I was thrown to the floor and when I opened my mouth to shout, the surrounding girls' screamed. Then the teacher was upon me, cramming her fingers down my throat, two fingers when the first didn't help, and she pumped my head from the back with her other hand. "Stand back, give him air—can't you see he's choking? Somebody get the nurse!"

"Is he dying?"

"What's all that stuff?"

What was her name—that second woman who had crammed something down my throat? I could see her perfectly. For fifty years she had been pale and prim and ever so respectable but I remember her as a hairy-nostriled and badly dentured banshee with fingers poisoned by furtive tobacco. I remember reaching out to paw her face to make her stop this impulsive assault on an innocent American, when suddenly I saw it: the blue rubble on my shirt, the bright sticky gobs of blue on the backs of my hands, the blue tint my eyes picked up off my cheeks. *I've been shot*, I thought. Blood is blue when you're really hurt. Then one of the boys let go of my arm and I was dropped to one elbow. "That's *ink*, Miss Carstairs. That's not blood or anything—that's *ink*. He was sucking his pen."

She finally looked closely at me, her eyes narrowing with reproach and disappointment. Her fingers fluttered in my throat. *Canadians!* I'd wanted to scream, *what do you want?* You throw me on the floor because of my accent and you pump your fingers in my throat fit to choke me then worst of all you start laughing when you find I'm not dying. *But I am.* Stop it. You stupid Yank with your stupid pen and the stupid cowboy hat on top and you sucking it like a baby. I rolled to my knees and coughed and retched out the clots of ink, then bulled my way through the rows of curious girls in their flannel jumpers who were making "ugh" sounds, and, head down because I didn't want anyone else to catch me and administer first aid, I dashed the two blocks to the Blankenship house in what, coatless, seemed like zero cold.

I let myself in the kitchen, quietly, to wash before I was seen. In the living room, a voice was straining, almost shouting. It wasn't my mother and I thought for an instant it might be Miss Carstairs who somehow had beaten me home. I moved closer.

"John says you're a bloody fool and I couldn't agree more!"

Aunt Valerie held a letter and she was snapping the envelope in my mother's face. "A bloody little fool, and that's not all—"

"I see I shouldn't have shown it to you."

"He's not worth it—here," she threw the letter in my mother's lap, "don't tell me that was the first time. *She was there*—doesn't that mean anything to you? *That woman* was there the whole time. How much do you think he cares for your feelings? Does he know how you felt when you got there—"

"No one will ever know."

"Well someone better make *you* know. I don't think you're competent. I think he's got a spell on you if you want my opinion. It's like a poison—"

"I'm not minimizing it," my mother broke in, and though she was sitting and didn't seem angry, her voice had risen and without straining it was blotting out my aunt's. "I'm not minimizing it. I know she wasn't the first and she might not be the last—"

"That's even more—"

"Will you let me finish? I didn't marry a Blankenship. You can tell my brother that I remember very well all the advice he gave me and my answer to all of you is that it's my life and I'm responsible and you can all . . ."

"Go . . . to . . . hell—is that it?"

"In so many words. Exactly. You can all go to hell."

Go to hell: I remember the way she said it, for she never said it again, not in my presence. More permission than a command: *yes, you may go to hell.* But it lifted Aunt Valerie out of her shoes.

"Now I *know!*" she cried. "I *see* it."

"See what?"

"What he's turned you into. One letter from him saying he wants you and you're running back—like a . . . like an I-don't-know-what! Only some things a woman can guess even when she doesn't want to. I don't deny he's a handsome devil. They all are. But to *degrade* yourself, really—"

Then my mother stood and looked at the door, straight at me, whom she must have seen. Her face was a jumble of frowns and smiles. I moved back toward the kitchen. "This will be our address," I heard her say. "Mrs. Mildred Thibidault."

She didn't come to the kitchen. She went upstairs, and Aunt Valerie stayed in the living room. I pictured her crying or cursing, throwing the porcelain off the mantel. I felt sorry for her; I understood her better than my mother. But minutes later she turned on the vacuum cleaner. And I returned quietly to the kitchen then slammed the outside door loudly and shouted, "I'm home, Aunt Valerie!" And then, knowing the role if not the words, I went upstairs to find out when we were leaving and where we would be going.

This long afternoon and evening, I closed my eyes and heard sounds of my childhood: the skipping rope slaps a dusty street in a warm southern twilight. The bats are out, the lightning bugs, the whip-poor-wills. I am the boy on yellow grass patting a hound, feeling him tremble under my touch. *Slap, slap,* a girl strains forward with her nose and shoulders, lets the rope *slap, slap, slap,* as she catches the rhythm before jumping in. The girls speed it up—hot pepper it's called—and they begin a song, something insulting about Negroes. The anonymous hound lays his head on my knee. Gnats encrust his eyes. *Poor dog,* I say. His breath is bad, his ears are frayed from fights, his eyes are moist and pink and tropical . . .

All day the slap, slap. The rope in a dusty yard, a little pit between the girls who turn it. As I walked today in another climate, now a man, I heard boots skipping on a wet city pavement, a girl running with her lover, a girl in a maxi-coat on a Montreal street. *Tschip-tschip:* I'd been listening for it, boots on sand over a layer of ice. A taxi waited at the corner, its wipers thrashing as the engine throbbed. And tonight, over the shallow breathing of my son, an aluminum shovel strikes the concrete, under new snow.

What can I make of this, I ask myself, staring now at the license plates on the wall. Five years ago in Wisconsin on a snowy evening like this, with our boy just a bundle in the middle of his crib, I looked out our bedroom window. Snow had been falling all that day, all evening too, and had just begun letting up. We were renting a corner house that year; my first teaching job. I was twenty-four and feeling important. I was political that year of the teach-in. I'd spoken out the day before and been abused by name on a local TV channel. A known agitator. Six inches of new snow had fallen. An hour later a policeman came to our door and issued a summons and twenty-dollar fine for keeping an uncleared walk.

America, I'd thought then. A friend called; he'd gotten a ticket too. Harassment—did I want to fight it? I said I'd think about it, but I knew suddenly that I didn't care.

Watching the police car stop at the corner and one policeman get out, kick his feet on our steps then hold his finger on the bell a full thirty seconds, I'd thought of other places we could be, of taking the option my parents had accidently left me. Nothing principled, nothing heroic, nothing even defiant. And so my son is skiing and learning French and someday he'll ask me why I made him do it, and he'll exercise the option we've accidentally left him . . . *slap-slap*, the dusty rope. Patrolmen on our steps, the shovel scraping a snowy walk.

I'm still a young man, but many things have gone for good.

A North American Education

Education

Eleven years after the death of Napoleon, in the presidency of Andrew Jackson, my grandfather, Boniface Thibidault, was born. For most of his life he was a *journalier*, a day laborer, with a few years off for wars and buccaneering. Then at the age of fifty, a father and widower, he left Paris and came alone to the New World and settled in Sorel, a few miles down river from Montreal. He worked in the shipyards for a year or two then married his young housekeeper, an eighteen-year-old named Lise Beaudette. Lise, my grandmother, had that resigned look of a Quebec girl marked early for a nursing order if marriage couldn't catch her, by accident, first. In twenty years she bore fifteen children, eight of them boys, five of whom survived. The final child, a son, was named Jean-Louis and given at birth to the Church. As was the custom with the last boy, he was sent to the monastery as soon as he could walk, and remained with the Brothers for a dozen years, taking his meals and instructions as an apprentice.

It would have been fitting if Boniface Thibidault, then nearly eighty, had earned a fortune in Sorel—but he didn't. Or if a son had survived to pass on his stories—but none were listening. Or if Boniface himself had written something—but he was illiterate. Boniface was cut out for something different. One spring morning in 1912, the man who had seen two child brides through menopause stood in the mud outside his cottage and defied Sorel's first horseless carriage to churn its way through the April muck to his door, and if by the Grace of God it did, to try going on while he, an old man, pushed it back downhill. Money was evenly divided on the man and the driver, whom Boniface also defamed for good measure. The driver was later acquitted of manslaughter in Sorel's first fatality and it was never ascertained if Boniface died of the bumping, the strain, or perhaps the shock of meeting his match. Jean-Louis wasn't there. He left the church a year later by walking out and never looking back. He was my father.

The death of Boniface was in keeping with the life, yet I think of my grandfather as someone special, a character from a well-packed novel who enters once and is never fully forgotten. I think of Flaubert's *Sentimental Education* and the porters who littered the decks of the *Ville-de-Montereau* on the morning of September 15, 1840, when young Frédéric Moreau was about to sail. My grandfather was already eight in 1840, a good age for cabin boys. But while Frédéric was about to meet Arnoux and his grand passion, Boniface was content to pocket a tip and beat it, out of the novel and back into his demimonde.

I have seen one picture of my grandfather, taken on a ferry between Quebec and Levis in 1895. He looks strangely like Sigmund Freud: bearded, straw-hatted, buttoned against the river breezes. It must have been a cold day—the vapor from the nearby horses steams in the background. As a young man he must have been, briefly, extraordinary. I think of him as a face in a Gold Rush shot, the one face that seems both incidental and immortal guarding a claim or watering a horse, the face that seems lifted from the crowd, from history, the face that could be dynastic.

And my father, Jean-Louis Thibidault, who became Gene and T. B. Doe—he too stands out in pictures. A handsome man, a contemporary man (and yet not even a man of this century. His original half-brothers back in France would now be 120 years old; he would be, by now, just seventy); a salesman and businessman. I still have many pictures, those my mother gave me. The earliest is of a strong handsome man with very short legs. He is lounging on an old canvas chaise under a maple tree, long before aluminum furniture, long before I was born. A scene north of Montreal, just after they were married. It is an impressive picture, but for the legs, which barely reach the grass. Later he would grow into his shortness, would learn the vanities of the short and never again stretch out casually, like the tall. In another picture I am standing with him on a Florida beach. I am five, he is forty-two. I am already the man I was destined to be; he is still the youth he always was. My mother must have taken the shot—I can tell, for I occupy the center—and it is one of those embarrassing shots parents often take. I am in my wet transparent underpants and I've just been swimming at Daytona Beach. It is 1946, our first morning in Florida. It isn't a vacation; we've arrived to start again, in the sun. The war is over, the border is open, the old black Packard is parked behind us. I had wanted to swim but had no trunks; my father took me down in my underwear. But in the picture my face is worried, my cupped hands are reaching down to cover myself, but I was late or the picture early—it seems instead that I am pointing to it, a fleshy little spot on my transparent pants. On the back of the picture my father had written:

> Thibidault et fils,
> Daytona, avr/46

We'd left Montreal four days before, with snow still gray in the tenements' shadow, the trees black and budless over the dingy winter street. Our destination was a town named Hartley where my father had a friend from Montreal who'd started a lawn furniture factory. My father was to become a traveling salesman for Laverdure's Lawn Laddies, and I was to begin my life as a salesman's son. As reader of back issues, as a collector of cancelled stamps (the inkier the better), as student and teacher of languages.

Thibidault et fils; Thibidault and son. After a week in Hartley I developed worms. My feet bled from itching and scratching. The worms were visible; I could prick them with pins. My mother took me to a clinic where the doctor sprayed my foot with a liquid freeze. Going on, the ice was pleasant, for Florida feet are always hot. Out on the bench I scraped my initials in the frost of my foot. It seemed right to me (before the pain of the thaw began); I was from Up North, the freezing was a friendly gesture for a Florida doctor. My mother held my foot between her hands and told me stories of her childhood, ice-skating for miles on the Battleford River in Saskatchewan, then riding home under fur rugs in a horse-drawn sleigh. Though she was the same age as my father, she was the eldest of six—somewhere between them was a missing generation. The next morning the itching was worse and half a dozen new worms radiated from the ball of my foot. My mother then consulted her old *Canadian Doctor's Home Companion*—my grandfather Blankenship had been a doctor, active for years in curling circles, Anglican missions, and crackpot Toryism—and learned that footworms, etc., were unknown in Canada but sometimes afflicted Canadian travelers in Tropical Regions. Common to all hot climes, the book went on, due to poor sanitation and the unspeakable habits of the non-white peoples, even in the Gulf Coast and Indian Territories of our southern neighbor. No known cure, but lack of attention can be fatal.

My mother called in a neighbor, our first contact with the slovenly woman who lived downstairs. She came up with a bottle of carbolic acid and another of alcohol, and poured the acid over the worms and told me to yell when it got too hot. Then with alcohol she wiped it off. The next morning my foot had peeled and the worms were gone. And I thought, inspecting my peeled, brown foot, that in some small way I had become less northern, less hateful to the kids around me though I still sounded strange and they shouted after me, "Yankee, Yankee!"

My father was already browned and already spoke with a passable southern accent. When he wasn't on the road with Lawn Laddies he walked around barefoot or in shower clogs. But he never got worms, and he was embarrassed that I had.

Thibidault and son: he was a fisherman and I always fished at his side. Fished for what? I wonder now—he was too short and vain a man to really be a fisherman. He dressed too well, couldn't swim, despised the taste of fish, shunned the cold, the heat, the bugs, the rain. And yet we fished every Sunday, wherever we lived. Canada, Florida, the Middle West, heedless as deer of crossing borders. The tackle box (oily childhood smell) creaked at our feet. The fir-lined shores and pink granite beaches of Ontario gleamed behind us. Every cast became a fresh hope, a trout or *doré* or even a muskie. But we never caught a muskie or a trout, just the snake-like fork-boned pike that we let go by cutting the line when the plug was swallowed deep. And in Florida, with my father in his Harry Truman shirts and sharkskin pants, the warm bait-well sloshing with half-dead shiners, we waited for bass and channel cat in Okeechobee, Kissimmee and a dozen other bug-beclouded lakes. Gar fish, those tropical pike, drifted by the boat. Gators churned in a narrow channel and dragonflies lit on my cane pole tip. And as I grew older and we came back North (but not all the way), I remember our Sundays in Cincinnati, standing shoulder-to-shoulder with a few hundred others around a clay-banked tub lit with arc-lamps. Scummy pay-lakes with a hot dog stand behind, a vision of hell for a Canadian or a Floridian, but we paid and we fished and we never caught a thing. Ten hours every Sunday from Memorial Day to Labor Day, an unquestioning ritual that would see me dress in my fishing khakis, race out early and buy the Sunday paper before we left (so I could check the baseball averages—what a normal kid I might have been!), then pack the tackle-box and portable radio (for the Cincinnati double-header) in the trunk. Then I would get my father up. He'd have his coffee and a few cigarettes then shout, "Mildred, Frankie and I are going fishing!" She would be upstairs reading or sewing. We were still living in a duplex; a few months later my parents were to start their furniture store and we would never fish again. We walked out, my father and I, nodding to the neighbors (a few kids, younger than I, asked if they could go, a few young fathers would squint and ask, "Not again, Gene?"); and silently we drove, and later, silently, we fished.

Then came a Sunday just before Labor Day when I was thirteen and we didn't go fishing. I was dressed for it and the car was packed as usual, but my father drove to the County Fair instead. Not the Hamilton County Fair in Cincinnati—we drove across the river into Boone County, Kentucky, where things were once again southern and shoddy.

I had known from the books and articles my mother was leaving in the bathroom, that I was supposed to be learning about sex. I'd read the books and figured out the anatomy for myself; I wondered only how to ask a girl for it and what to do once I got there. Sex was something like dancing, I supposed, too intricate and spontaneous for a boy like me. And so we toured the Fair Grounds that morning, saying nothing, reviewing the prize sows and heifers, watching a stock-car race and a miniature rodeo. I could tell from my father's breathing, his coughing, his attempt to put his arm around my shoulder, that this was the day he was going to talk to me about sex, the facts of life, and the thought embarrassed him as much as it did me. I wanted to tell him to never mind; I didn't need it, it was something that selfish people did to one another.

He led me to a remote tent far off the fairway. There was a long male line outside, men with a few boys my age, joking loudly and smelling bad. My father looked away, silent. So this is the place, I thought, where I'm going to see it, going to learn something good and dirty, something they couldn't put on those Britannica Films and show in school. The sign over the entrance said only: *Princess Hi-Yalla. Shows Continuously.*

There was a smell, over the heat, over the hundred men straining for a place, over the fumes of pigsties and stockyards. It was the smell of furtiveness, rural slaughter and unquenchable famine. The smell of boy's rooms in the high school. The smell of sex on the hoof. The "Princess" on the runway wore not a stitch, and she was already lathered like a racehorse from her continuous dance. There was no avoiding the bright pink lower lips that she'd painted; no avoiding the shrinking, smiling, puckering, wrinkled labia. "Kiss, baby?" she called out, and the men went wild. The lips smacked us softly. The Princess was more a dowager, and more black than brown or yellow. She bent forward to watch herself, like a ventriloquist with a dummy. I couldn't turn away as my father had; it seemed less offensive to watch her wide flat breasts instead, and to think of her as another native from the *National Geographic*. She asked a guard for a slice of gum, then held it over the first row. "Who gwina wet it up fo' baby?" And a farmer licked both sides while his friends made appreciative noises, then handed it back. The Princess inserted it slowly, as though it hurt, spreading her legs like the bow-legged rodeo clown I'd seen a few minutes earlier. Her lower mouth chewed, her abdomen heaved, and she doubled forward to watch the progress. "Blow a bubble!" the farmer called, his friends screamed with laughter. But a row of boys in overalls, my age, stared at the woman and didn't smile. Nothing would amaze them—they were waiting for a bubble. Then she cupped her hand underneath and gum came slithering out. "Who wants this?" she called, holding it high, and men were whistling and throwing other things on the stage: key rings, handkerchiefs, cigarettes. She threw the gum toward us—I remember ducking as it came my way, but someone caught it. "Now then," she said, and her voice was as loud as a gospel singer's, "baby's fixin' to have herself a cig'rette." She walked to the edge of the stage (I could see her moist footprints in the dust), her toes curled over the side. "Which of you men out there is givin' baby a cig'-rette?" Another farmer standing behind his fat adolescent son threw up two cigarettes. The boy, I remember, was in overalls and had the cretinous look of fat boys in overalls: big, sweating, red-cheeked, with eyes like calves' in a roping event. By the time I looked back on stage, the Princess had inserted the cigarette and had thrust baby out over the runway and was asking for matches. She held the match herself. And the cigarette glowed, smoke came out, an ash formed . . .

I heard moaning, long low moans, and I felt the eyes of a dozen farmers leap to the boy in overalls. He was jumping and whimpering and the men were laughing as he tried to dig into his sealed-up pants. Forgetting the buttons at his shoulders, he was holding his crotch as though it burned. He was running in place, moaning, then screaming, "Daddy!" and I forgot about the Princess. Men cleared a circle around him and began clapping and chanting, "Whip it out!" and the boy was crying, "Daddy, I cain't hold it back no more!"

My father grabbed me then by the elbow, and said, "Well, have you seen enough?" The farm boy had collapsed on the dirt floor, and was twitching on his back as though a live wire were passed through his body. A navy-blue stain that I thought was blood was spreading between his legs. I thought he'd managed to pull his penis off. My father led me out and he was mad at me for something—it was *me* who had brought him there, and his duties as my father—and just as we stepped from the tent I yelled, "Wait—it's happening to me too." I wanted to cry with embarrassment for I hadn't felt any urgency before entering the tent. It seemed like a sudden, irresistible need to urinate, something I couldn't hold back. But worse than water; something was ripping at my crotch. My light-colored fishing khakis would turn brown in water, and the dark stain was already forming.

"Jesus Christ—are you *sick*? That was an old woman —how could *she* . . . how could *you* . . ." He jerked me forward by the elbow. "Jesus God," he muttered, pulling me along down the fairway, then letting me go and walking so fast I had to run, both hands trying to cup the mess I had made. Thousands of people passed me, smiling, laughing. "I don't know about you," my father said. "*I think there's something wrong with you*," and it was the worse thing my father could say about me. We were in the car. I was crying in the back seat. "Don't tell me someone didn't see you—didn't you think of that? Or what if a customer saw *me*—but you didn't think of that either, did you? Here I take you to something I thought you'd like, something any *normal* boy would like, and—"

I'd been afraid to talk. The wetness was drying, a stain remained. "You know Murray Lieberman?" my father asked a few minutes later.

"The salesman?"

"He has a kid your age and so we were talking—"

"Never mind." I said.

"Well, what in the name of God is wrong with two fathers getting together, eh? It was supposed to *show* you what it's like, about women, I mean. It's better than any drawing, isn't it? You want books all the time? You want to *read* about it, or do you want to see it? At least now you *know*, so go ahead and read. Tell your mother we were fishing today, O.K.? And *that*—that was a Coke you spilled, all right?"

And no other talk, man-to-man, or father-to-son, had ever taken place.

I think back to Boniface Thibidault—how would he, how *did* he, show his sons what to do and where to do it? He was a Frenchman, not a North American; he learned it in Paris, not in a monastery as my father had. And I am, partially at least, a Frenchman too. My father should have taken me to a *cocotte*, to his own mistress perhaps, for the initiation, *la déniasement*. And I, in my own love-making, would have forever honored him. But this is North America and my father, despite everything, was in his silence a Quebec Catholic of the nineteenth century. Sex, despite my dreams of something better, something nobler, still smells of the circus tent, of something raw and murderous. Other kinds of sex, the adjusted, contented, fulfilling sex of school and manual, seems insubstantial, willfully ignorant of the depths.

At thirteen I was oldest of eighty kids on the block, a thankless distinction, and my parents at fifty had a good twenty years on the next oldest, who, it happened, shared our duplex.

There lived on that street, and I was beginning to notice in that summer before the sideshow at the county fair, several girl brides and one or two maturely youthful wives. The brides, under twenty and with their first or second youngsters, were a sloppy crew who patrolled the street in cut-away shorts and bra-less elasticized halters that had to be pulled up every few steps. They set their hair so tightly in pin curlers that the effect, at a distance, was of the mange. Barefoot they pushed their baby

[173]

strollers, thighs sloshing as they walked, or sat on porch furniture reading movie magazines and holding tinted plastic baby bottles between their knees. Though they sat in the sun all day they never tanned. They were spreading week by week while their husbands, hard athletic gas-pumpers, played touch football on the street every Sunday.

But there were others; in particular the wife next door, our two floors being mirror images of the other, everything back-to-back but otherwise identical. What was their name? She was a fair woman, about thirty, with hair only lightly bleached and the kind of figure that one first judges slightly too plump until something voluptuous in her, or you, makes you look again and you see that she is merely extraordinary; a full woman who had once been a lanky girl. She had three children, two of them girls who favored the husband, but I can't quite place his name or face. Her name was Annette.

She was French. That had been a point of discussion once. Born in Maine, she would often chat with my father in what French she remembered while her husband played football or read inside. By that time I had forgotten most of my French. And now I remember the husband. His name was Lance—Lance!—and he was dark, square-shouldered, with a severe crewcut that sliced across an ample bald spot. He traveled a lot; I recall him sitting in a lawn chair on summer evenings, reading the paper and drinking a beer till the mosquitoes drove him in.

And that left Annette alone, and Annette had no friends on the block. She gave the impression, justified, of far outdistancing the neighborhood girls. Perhaps she frightened them, being older and by comparison, a goddess. She would sit on a lawn chair in the front yard, on those male-less afternoons of toddling children and cranky mothers and was so stunning in a modest sundress that I would stay inside and peek at her through a hole I had cut in the curtains. Delivery trucks, forced to creep through the litter of kids and abandoned toys, lingered longer than they had to, just to look. At thirteen I could stare for hours, unconscious of peeping, unaware, really, of what I wanted or expected to see. It was almost like fishing, with patience and anticipation keeping me rooted.

My parents were at the new property, cleaning it up for a grand opening. I was given three or four dollars a day for food and I'd spend fifty or sixty cents of it on meaty and starchy grease down at the shopping center. I was getting fat. Every few days I carried a bulging pocketful of wadded bills down to the bank and cashed them for a ten or twenty. And the bills would accumulate in my wallet. I was too young to open an account without my parents' finding out; the question was how to spend it. After a couple of weeks I'd go downtown and spend astounding sums, for a child, on stamps.

While I was in the shopping center I began stealing magazines from the drugstore. The scandal mags, the Hollywood parties, the early *Playboy* and its imitators —I stole because I was too good to be seen buying them. I placed them between the pages of the *Sporting News*, which I also read cover-to-cover, then dropped a wadded five-dollar bill in the newspaper honor box, raced home, and feasted. Never one for risks, I burned the residue or threw them out in a neighbor's garbage can, my conscience clear for a month's more stealing and secret reading. There was never a time in my life when sex had been so palpable; when the very sight of any girl vaguely developed or any woman up to forty and still in trim could make my breath come short, make my crotch tingle under my baggy pants. In the supermarket, when young mothers dipped low to pick a carton of Cokes from the bottom shelf, I dipped with them. When the counter girl at the drugstore plunged her dipper in the ice cream tub, I hung over the counter to catch a glimpse of her lacy bra; when the neighbor women hung out their clothes, I would take the stairs two at a time to watch from above. When those young wives hooked their thumbs under the knitted elastic halters and gave an upward tug, I let out a little whimper. How close it was to madness; how many other fat thirteen- and fourteen-year-olds with a drop more violence, provocation, self-pity or whatever, would plunge a knife sixty times into those bellies, just to run their fingers inside the shorts and peel the halter back, allowing the breasts to ooze aside? And especially living next to Annette whose figure made flimsy styles seem indecent and modest dresses maddening. Her body possessed the clothes too greedily, sucked the material to her flesh. She was the woman, I now realize, that Dostoyevski and Kazantzakis and even Faulkner knew; a Grushenka or the young village widow, a dormant body that kindled violence.

The duplexes were mirror images with only the staircases and bathrooms adjoining. In the summer with Annette at home, her children out playing or taking a nap, her husband away, or just at work, she took many baths. From wherever I sat in our duplex watching television or reading my magazines, I could hear the drop of the drain plug in her bathroom, the splash of water rushing in, the quick expansion of the hot water pipes.

I could imagine the rest, exquisitely. First testing the water with her finger, then drying the finger on her shorts and then letting them drop. Testing the water again before unhooking the bra in a careless sweep and with another swipe, peeling off her panties. The thought of Annette naked, a foot away, made the walls seem paper-thin, made the tiles grow warm. Ear against the tiles I could hear the waves she made as she settled back, the squeaking of her heels on the bottom of the tub as she straightened her legs, the wringing of a face cloth, plunk of soap as it dropped. The scene was as vivid, with my eyes closed and my hot ear on the warm tile, as murders on old radio shows. I thought of the childhood comic character who could shrink himself with magic sand; how for me that had always translated itself into watching the Hollywood starlets from their bathroom heating registers. But Annette was better or at least as good, and so available. If only there were a way, a shaft for midgets. It wasn't right to house strangers so intimately without providing a way to spy. I looked down to the tile floor—a crack? Something a bobby pin could be twisted in, just a modest, modest opening? And I saw the pipes under the sink, two slim swannecks, one for hot, one for cold, that cut jaggedly through the tile wall—they had to connect! Then on my hands and knees I scraped away the plaster that held the chromium collar around the pipe. As I had hoped, the hole was a good quarter-inch wider than the pipes and all that blocked a straight-on view of the other bathroom were the collars on Annette's pipes. It would be nothing to punch my way through, slide the rings down, and lie on the tile floor in the comfort of my own bathroom and watch it all; Annette bathing! Ring level was below the tub, but given the distance the angle might correct itself. But detection would be unbearable; if caught I'd commit suicide. She was already out of the bath (but there'll be other days, I thought). She took ten-minute baths (how much more could a man bear?), the water was draining and now she was running the lavatory faucet which seemed just over my head. How long before she took another bath? It would seem, now that I had a plan, as long as the wait between issues of my favorite magazines.

I rested on the floor under the sink until Annette left her bathroom. Then I walked down to the shopping center and had a Coke to steady myself. I bought a nailfile. When I got back Annette was sitting in her yard, wearing a striped housedress and looking, as usual, fresh from a bath. I said hello and she smiled very kindly. Then I turned my door handle and cried, "Oh, no!"

"What is it, Frankie?" she asked, getting up from her chair.

"I left my key inside."

"Shall I call your father?"

"No," I said, "I think I can get in through the window. But could I use your bathroom first?"

"Of course."

I checked upstairs for kids. Then I locked myself inside and with the new file, scraped away the plaster and pulled one collar down. Careful as always, aware that I would make a good murderer or a good detective, I cleaned up the plaster crumbs. I'd forgotten to leave our own bathroom light on, but it seemed that I could see all the way through. Time would tell. *Take a bath,* I willed her, as I flushed the toilet. It reminded me of fishing as a child, trying to influence the fish to bite. It's very hot, sticky, just right for a nice cool bath . . . My own flesh was stippled, I shivered as I stepped outside and saw her again. She'd soon be *mine*—something to do for the rest of the summer! My throat was so tense I couldn't even thank her. I climbed inside through the living-room window that I had left open.

I took the stairs two at a time, stretched myself out under the sink to admire the job. I'd forgotten to leave *her* light on, but I thought I could see the white of her tub in the darkened bathroom, and even an empty tub was enough to sustain me.

How obvious was the pipe and collar? It suddenly seemed blatant, that she would enter the bathroom, undress, sit in the tub, turn to the wall, and scream. Do a peeper's eyes shine too brightly? In school I'd often been able to stare a kid into turning around—it was now an unwanted gift.

You're getting warm again, Annette. Very very hot. You want another bath. You're getting up from the chair, coming inside, up the stairs . . . I kept on for hours till it was dark. I heard the kids taking baths and saw nothing. The white of the bathtub was another skin of plaster, no telling how thick. I'd been cheated.

Another day. There had to be another link—I had faith that the builders of duplexes were men who provided, out of guilt, certain amenities. Fans were in the ceiling. Windows opened on the opposite sides, the heating ducts were useless without a metal drill. Only the medicine cabinets were left. They had to be back-to-back. I opened ours, found the four corner screws, undid them, took out the medicines quietly (even my old Florida carbolic acid), then eased the chest from its plaster nest. It worked. I was facing the metal backing of Annette's medicine chest. The fit was tight and I could never take a chance of tampering with hers—what if I gave it a nudge when Lance was shaving and the whole thing came crashing down, revealing me leaning over my sink in the hole where our medicine chest had been?

The used-razor slot. A little slot in the middle. I popped the paper coating with the nailfile. I darkened our own bathroom. If Annette opened her chest, I'd see her. But would she open it with her clothes off? Was she tall enough to make it count? How many hours would I have to stand there, stretched over the sink, waiting, and could I, every day, put the chest back up and take it down without some loud disaster? What if my father came home to shave, unexpectedly?

I waited all afternoon and all evening and when eight o'clock came I ended the vigil and put the chest back up.

With a desire so urgent, there *had* to be a way of pene-
trating an inch and a half of tile and plaster. When she
was in her bath I felt I could have devoured the walls
between us. Anything *heard* so clearly had to yield to
vision—that was another natural law—just as anything
dreamt had to become real, eventually.

I became a baby-sitter; the oldest kid on the block,
quiet and responsible. I watched television in nearly
every duplex on the street, ignored the whimpers, filled
bottles, and my pockets bulged with more unneeded
cash. I poked around the young parents' bedrooms and
medicine cabinets, only half-repelled by the clutter and
unfamiliar odors, the stickiness, the grayness of young
married life in a Midwest suburb. I found boxes of pro-
phylactics in top drawers and learned to put one on and
to walk around with it on until the lubrication stuck to
my underwear. Sex books and nudist magazines showing
pubic hair were stuffed in nightstands, and in one or
two homes I found piles of home-made snaps of the
young wife when she'd been slim and high school
young, sitting naked in the sun, in a woods somewhere.
She'd been posed in dozens of ways, legs wide apart,
fingers on her pubic hair, tongue curled between her
teeth. Others of her, and of a neighbor woman, on the
same living-room sofa that I was sitting on: fatter now,
her breasts resting on a roll of fat around her middle,
her thighs shadowed where the skin had grown soft.
This is the girl I see every day, pushing that carriage,
looking like a fat girl at a high school hang-out. Those
bigger girls in my school, in bright blue sweaters, ear-

rings, black curly hair, bad skin, black corduroy jackets, smoking. They become like this; they *are* like this.

These were the weeks in August, when my mother was leaving the articles around. Soon my father would take me to the county fair. There were no answers to the questions I asked, holding those snapshots, looking again (by daylight) at the wife (in ragged shorts and elastic halter) who had consented to the pictures. They were like murder victims, the photos were like police shots in the scandal magazines, the women looked like mistresses of bandits. There was no place in the world for the life I wanted, for the pure woman I would some-day, somehow, marry.

I baby-sat for Annette and Lance, then for Annette alone, and I worked again on the lavatory scheme, the used-razor slot, and discovered the slight deficiencies in the architecture that had thrown my calculations off. I could see from their bathroom into ours much better than I could ever see into theirs. Annette kept a neat house and life with her, even I could appreciate, must have been a joy of lust and efficiency, in surroundings as clean and attractive as a *Playboy* studio.

One evening she came over when my parents were working, to ask me to baby-sit for a couple of hours. Lance wasn't in. Her children were never a problem and though it was a week night and school had begun, I agreed. She left me a slice of Lance's birthday cake, and begged me to go to sleep in case she was late.

An hour later, after some reading, I used her bathroom, innocently. If only I lived here, with Annette over there! I opened her medicine chest to learn some more about her: a few interesting pills "for pain," Tampex Super (naturally, I thought), gauze and adhesive, something for piles (for him, I hoped). And then I heard a noise from our bathroom; I heard our light snap on. My parents must have come home early.

I knew from a cough that it wasn't my mother. The Thibidault medicine chest was opened. I peered through the razor slot and saw young fingers among our bottles, blond hair and a tanned forehead: Annette. She picked out a jar, then closed the door. I fell to the floor and put my eye against the pipes. Bare golden legs. Then our light went out.

I looked into our bathroom for the next few seconds then ran to Annette's front bedroom where the youngest girl slept, and pressed over her crib to look out the window. She was just stepping out and walking slowly to the station wagon of Thibidault Furniture, which had been parked. She got in the far side and the car immediately, silently, backed away, with just its parking lights on . . .

And that was all. For some reason, perhaps the shame of my complicity, I never asked my father why he had come home or why Annette had been in our bathroom. I didn't have to—I'd gotten a glimpse of Annette, which was all I could handle anyway. I didn't understand the rest. *Thibidault et fils*, fishing again.

Jean-Louis Thibidault, twice-divorced, is dead; buried in Venice, Florida. Bridge of Sighs Cemetery. I even asked his widow if I could have him removed to Sorel, Quebec. She didn't mind, but the *prêtre-vicaire* of my father's old parish turned me down. When my father was born, Venice, Florida, was five miles offshore and fifty feet underwater. The thought of him buried there tortures my soul.

There was another Sunday in Florida. A hurricane was a hundred miles offshore and due to strike Fort Lauderdale within the next six hours. We drove from our house down Las Olas to the beach (Fort Lauderdale was still an inland city then), and parked half a mile away, safe from the paint-blasting sand. We could hear the breakers under the shriek of the wind, shaking the wooden bridge we walked on. Then we watched them crash, brown with weeds and suspended sand. And we could see them miles offshore, rolling in forty feet high and flashing their foam like icebergs. A few men in swimming suits and woolen sweaters were standing in the crater pools, pulling out the deep-sea fish that had been stunned by the trip and waves. Other fish littered the beach, their bellies blasted by the change in pressure. My mother's face was raw and her glasses webbed with salt. She went back to the car on her own. My father and I sat on the bench for another hour and I could see behind his crusty sunglasses. His eyes were moist and dancing, his hair stiff and matted. We sat on the bench until we were soaked and the municipal guards rounded us up. Then they barricaded the boulevards and we went back to the car, the best day of fishing we'd ever had, and we walked hand in hand for the last time, talking excitedly, dodging coconuts, power lines, and shattered glass, feeling brave and united in the face of the storm. My father and me. What a day it was, what a once-in-a-lifetime day it was.

Snow People

A Novella

1

One moment there were girls jumping
rope in the dust, his friends pounding their mitts and
George Stewart waving his bat, and the next he was
wandering out beyond second base with a ringing in
his ears, his nose smelling bone and all his side-vision
gone. George was the first to walk beside him, maybe
because he was the oldest, too old to be playing hardball
with nine- and ten-year-olds. Maybe also because George
Stewart had saved his life the summer before when
he'd paddled beyond the pier in Oshacola Lake on an
old inner tube through which he had somehow slipped
into a roar of bubbles. He had saved him then; now
it was George, the boy felt, who had somehow killed
him.

"Walk it off, you'll be O.K."

"Where'd it hit you at?"

He didn't know. He couldn't talk—in the throat perhaps? He was walking, pitched to one side and

leaning hard on George Stewart. He walked across the red dirt road where the fine clay dust felt cool on his feet, up the driveway to the porch door, bursting camphor berries as he walked. The door off the porch was locked.

"Ain't they home?" George asked. The truck was gone. *I must have cut my mouth,* he thought, for his T-shirt was pink from drool. It was the first time he'd ever been badly hurt, but where was it coming from? His chest? His nose?

"Ain't you got a key even?"

He was a boy entrusted with keys, always had been. There was a key to the house since his parents had started a small furniture factory and were usually out working at it, and there were other keys kept on a ring around his belt-loop; some to the factory buildings and others to apartments and houses they'd rented and vacated over the years.

"I'll be O.K.," he said, his first words, and a pink blood bubble built as he spoke. Inside, the house was stale and humid but a little cooler than it would have been with the windows open. He found himself in the bathroom, still with George Stewart and maybe some others, sweating and shivering, bent over the toilet bowl while a pink film spread on the water. He vomited, but it came out his nose because his mouth wouldn't open. Only the smell and residue of talcum powder and the yellow carton of Serutan on the toilet ledge assured him that he was home, in a bathroom unlike anyone else's, especially in Florida.

The pain was locating itself: in the back of his neck,

in his nose, in his jaw. He wondered how a baseball, like a bullet, could do all that at once.

"You can have my ups," said George Stewart, who'd run the bases before helping him. "You better wipe all that up with a towel." He took the nearest at hand, a white one that his father used, but the boy rejected it. He used toilet paper instead. Blood, his mother always said, left a permanent stain.

In the mirror, after washing, he stared at an unknown face. Baked pink over his cheeks and nose—he'd been out too long in the late August sun—but then the dark, dried lips and lump in his cheek and jaw. Pink drool ran from the corner of his mouth.

"Going back?"

"I don't think I can." Through clenched teeth his voice reminded him of the morons in his class, the fifteen-year-olds who once in a while attempted to answer a question. He wondered if the blow on the head had made him a moron. He wanted to sleep, he thought of trappers caught in a blizzard, but if he slept would he ever wake up?

Not that dying was such a bad thing. The summer before, he'd picked up a cube of rat poison from under the sink, dark and tempting as a chocolate caramel, unwrapped it and held it in his hand until it got soft. Then he'd licked his fingers and gone to bed with a letter to his mother under the pillow saying that he'd done it out of curiosity and that he wasn't mad at her for anything (he knew she'd take it personally); she shouldn't feel that there was anything he'd wanted and couldn't have, or that there was anything she could have done to save him. He'd arranged his room neatly, dressed himself in school clothes, assigned his valuables to friends, then fallen asleep. When he awakened the next morning he'd felt grateful for the immortality he now indisputably possessed. By the time he remembered to retrieve the letter it had disappeared, though his mother never mentioned it.

So he shouldn't worry. He lay down on his cot in the back porch, under the screens where the bugs plopped at night. His head was pounding with each heartbeat, his vision throbbed, and his jaw ached. Then he slept, knowing he would wake, for he was immortal.

A week later he found himself in Orlando, three hours in a dentist's chair while his mouth was wired shut. Now he sounded like Zerlene the moron who lifted her skirts for the older boys. He had to eat by reaming crumbled food through the gap where his wisdom teeth would someday grow. He learned to manipulate a straw and to strain un-iced Cokes through his locked front teeth. He stood behind the teacher at recess, for to play anything was to risk an elbow, an errant bounce, or even the need for a sudden gulp of air. And so, standing behind the teacher as a junior referee, he found a niche that had been waiting for him though he hadn't known it; how much better it was, keeping track of his classmates' performances, carrying a rulebook and whistle, than trying himself against physical odds that were obvious if unadmitted. He was a reader and speller and if it had not been a southern school where science and arithmetic lagged behind, he'd have been a wizard there too. His place slightly behind second base or at the top of the concrete keyhole, at the teacher's side with whistle and rulebook, was proper, though he didn't know it yet.

For perhaps a month it worked. The kids accepted him as an incompetent who had tried, who was slow and ball-shy and easy to fake but didn't mind getting chosen last. But after a month of hot September games (he had two more weeks before the wires were due to come off), they began to associate him with the grade-book he carried and the imperious whistle he'd learned to blow with limited wind while pointing his finger at a foul, an out, or a questionable tag. He'd become a freak, and it was an isolated school in the dusty pine flats of northern Florida and a few of the kids remembered that he hadn't been born among them and no one knew of a church he attended, if any, and there was talk that his parents sounded *really* funny and ran a factory out at the old airport so he must be rich too, and no one appreciated his reading or the dates he knew in history and the way he won the spelling bee against sixth graders and the capitals he knew of all the states and that he wore shoes in the classroom instead of leaving them on the steps outside. Their judgment was swift. If they could, they would have killed him. But being boys of nine and ten, they knew they couldn't really kill. They could only hurt. The boy was like someone in a wheelchair or on crutches—just asking for it.

It started one day at the bicycle racks. It was three o'clock, the temperature up around ninety degrees, the bicycles scalding to the touch. They drew their bikes in a circle under a tree to let them cool. When he came out they didn't let him join their circle; he stood in the sun balancing the bike by a sticky rubber handgrip, putting his books on the seat. He wasn't that good on a bike, they knew that, and they suddenly hated him more for that than anything. They knew his route home, the dusty road where the ball field stood, even his house just across. A few boys started off in his general direction, taking the back streets to come out on the cement part of the Dixie Highway at South Street, before the clay stretch where he lived. It was a thrill, organizing an ambush with maps drawn in the sand, like a well-executed passing play—"run out for one, you go deep and you go short and I'll throw it here, at the X"—and the "X" would be where South Street cut off from the Dixie Highway in front of Chambers's General Store. In fact, they planned to have themselves a couple of Cokes inside as soon as it was over.

The boy knew it too. He knew they were after him and that the plan was complicated and somehow exciting, and he was excited too, being the victim. He simply didn't know how to avoid it. His parents were working at the factory and he was the boy entrusted with keys, nine years old and jingling like a janitor on his bike. He knew something was headed his way, like a football thrown right at him. He put on his pants-clip and pedaled off, the hot seat burning, his books bouncing, and the keys jiggling from his belt loop, down the Dixie Highway past the lake and high school and the Fair Grounds and baseball stadium, turning at Chambers's Store where the Greyhounds stopped and picked up the insolent young men with baseball gloves and cleated shoes who had failed to make the team. He started to breathe easier when he saw the dust ahead, and the red tire tracks in the hissing blacktop that was about to end.

They strung it just a little low for what they'd intended; they'd meant to catch him around the mouth or neck with the cat-gut line. As it was, with him not going fast and the line tangling first in the bike's basket, then popping up to catch him flush in the chest before snapping, two of the boys sliced their hands enough to yell from the bushes. But for the others it was beautiful, a little reminiscent of the Cisco Kid knocking a posse off their horses. The bike reared up like a stallion and the kid slipped off backward so fast they thought someone else had hooked him from the rear instead of sweeping him off his seat, and he was down on the pavement with the bike skittering for a second or two on just its back wheel before crashing down right on top of him. It didn't look like he was ever going to get up or even begin to cry, which wasn't too loud anyway in that closed-mouthed way of his, and there seemed to be a lot of blood, which frightened them enough to tell Mrs. Chambers about a kid who had fallen off his bike in the middle of the road. And then they lit out, back down the Dixie Highway past the high school and the Fair Grounds to their own parts of town, which were older and cooler and better shaded.

Most of the cuts were superficial, the usual scrapes on the elbow, banged knees. The knees of his pants were both ripped out and there would be bruises where the basket and handlebars had come dropping down. The bad cuts were in the mouth, where for the second time in a month the boy tasted blood and smelled the bone and gristle, but now it was worse, for the wires were sprung and came bristling through his lips and tongue and this time the blood was bright as it dripped off the ends of the wire onto the pavement. Mrs. Chambers helped him inside. She didn't know what had happened. First she guessed he'd eaten something that had exploded, or that someone had stuffed a pin cushion in his mouth—both perhaps serving him right for some thoughtless prank—and the boy couldn't talk because the wires would cut him up worse if he tried. It was a general store and well-equipped with the semi-rural exigencies of farmers and fishermen, and Henry Chambers went to the back and found some small wire-cutters and commenced to pruning the boy's mouth and lips, working the lips out over the ends he'd cut, then keeping them lifted while he worked inside, twisting and clipping while the boy screamed and kicked the counters fit to break the glass on top.

"What I can't understand is how he picked up all that wire in the first place," said Henry Chambers, a speculative man in a simple trade, and it was he who finally suggested calling a doctor. By that time the front of the boy's shirt looked like he'd spilled a Cherry Smash, or been shot, but the doctor, when he came, congratulated Henry for keeping cool in an emergency. As he cleaned the wounds, he told them all a story about coming across a nigger farmer who'd had his stomach slashed open by a harrow up in Georgia. The man was laying in his fields with about twenty feet of intestine in his lap spilling out into the dirt. "All you can do is work with what you got," said the doctor, who had cleaned off what he could with some Coke and then commenced to stuffing the guts back in, cramming them in elbow deep while the nigger sat there calmly enough, everything considered, smoking some of the doctor's Lucky Strikes. And he lived—couldn't no mule, couldn't no dog hit out on a highway live with half his guts sticking out, the doctor said—but that man hitched his overalls up and got into the doctor's car and was dropped at the closest nigger hospital and they sewed him up and he was back in his fields inside of a month. But the doctor, who told the story while cleaning out the boy's mouth with antiseptic, was a careful man, not the kind to belittle an honest injury, and the boy felt his was respectable enough to rank (being white and only a boy) with that of the farmer in the field but not, perhaps, of the same magnitude. The doctor asked him about the broken jaw he'd obviously suffered, and how long the wires had been on. "You're going to have to start from scratch," he said, and then he took him back to his clinic for more cleaning and clipping and since now at least the boy could speak, however weakly, he had him call his parents to explain what he thought had happened.

A week later, freshly wired in Orlando, and lectured to by the unforgiving orthodontist about playing dangerous games with a wired-shut jaw, the boy was back in school. He later tried to guess exactly what they had done that day when the bike suddenly bucked and he found himself bleeding on the pavement. He checked the spot, so indelibly marked with his blood—but found not a blemish on the surface. Perhaps it was something in the spokes, or in the chain. Whatever it was, it took on the aspect of a general principle with the boy, that whatever the comforting vision before him—that of the girls skipping rope and his team shouting encouragement behind him, or having finished a day in school without a headache and being only a minute from curling up on the sofa with "The Game of the Day" and a cold Coke, something dreadful could suddenly cut him down without warning. Or not quite without warning: without defense.

So life was unsafe even if he was the most careful boy in the school, who calculated risks before jumping in, whose older parents were more careful than those of the other kids, or so it seemed to him. He'd never seen his father drunk and his parents were too busy with the factory to have any friends in town. There was always something unsafe about other people's lives, their accidents and needless gashes, the way small kids ran around with knives and scissors, and broken bottles glittered in their yards. Their outhouses were never limed out, the stench mingling with unventilated cooking gas and boiled collard greens. He'd always pitied the kids who had little chance of growing up without scars or missing fingers, like the men who worked at his father's factory, all of whom were missing something. Yet it seemed, for all his caution, that he was the one who carried the scars.

He gave up officiating. He had permission to walk

around the building during recess, or to stay in the room and wash the boards if he wished, and he did. He was a third grader, an almost perfect reader who had polished off the year's book on the first night of classes, and had been attending to other things after school— the various magazines that came to the house: *Time*, *National Geographic*, *Maclean's* and the *Reader's Digest* that went directly to the bathroom to accumulate the talcum, spent hairs and grains of Serutan. On his wall he'd hung the maps of the Geographic Society, and on the dining room table after school he would copy out the Walter Weber wild-life paintings, committing them all to memory. He knew the capitals, all the capitals, and he knew the birds and fish of Florida. He was as good at copying as he was on statistics. On dozens of sheets of the factory's letterhead he copied bloody scenes from the Everglades, or cavemen stoning a mammoth, accompanied till dinnertime by the baseball broadcasts from chilly Fenway. At night, after his mother had come home to cook him his supper and then gone back to the factory, he'd take out his baseball bat and stand in the living room, swishing with each reported pitch to their local, last-place, hitters in a Class D entry.

One day in class after the jaw had healed but before he'd rejoined his classmates in games, or the teacher at the periphery, a strange thing happened. Normally when they studied geography, he and the teacher would carry on a dialogue about whatever state or country was being studied, its rivers, mountains, cities and products. In his private travels he had gone to whatever country was being discussed, had placed himself on the pre-war streets from the pictures in their old geography text, creating the world afresh with his own pronunciations of impossible names: Traffel-gar and Gibb-ral-tar. Veena and Pra-goo.

The teacher was talking that day of the great rivers of North America and the subject was the St. Lawrence which, she said, she'd once seen for herself in Cuebeck, Canada. She passed some photos around the class. The boy was about to raise his hand, but she went on about the trip she'd taken through Cuebeck, out on the Gasp Peninsula, and the boy found himself standing up—the teacher noticed, but she went on talking about the mountains in Gasp—and she asked if anyone could find them on the map. The boy was now walking slowly to the front of the class, and the teacher watched him from the corner of her eye, thinking that he should have asked permission to be excused, but it would be all right, this once.

"And they have a big rock at the end of Gasp called Purse Rock because it looks like a giant handbag stuck out in the ocean—" and then the boy picked up a piece of chalk and tapped the board for attention. "*C'n'est pas vrai*," he cried, writing quickly, "*Percé=Per-say*" and "*Gaspé=Gas-pay*." He tapped the first word. "*Ça veut dire un p'tit trou. Comme les Nez-Percés, les indiens. Ils ont un p'tit trou dans le nez . . .*" and he was smiling now, pointing to the side of his nose, looking around for other kids to laugh with him. "Don't you know the Indian tribes? Crows, Blackfeet, Shoshone? Nez Percé? *Percé, ça signifie comme ça—*" and he began to draw an Indian in full headdress on a white pony, one of his best copies from Holling C. Holling's *Book of the Indians*, when he turned with the first laughs from his classmates. "*Un instant—*" he started to say, thinking himself at home, drawing something for his father to see, playing the geography games they sometimes played, when the teacher stepped between him and the class and with the thick paddle he'd often seen her use on the morons, brought it down first on his arm, scattering the chalk, then on his flank, spinning him around so she could catch him by the collar, which ripped, and with one hand, bent him just enough to administer five of the hardest she'd ever delivered, on any boy for whatever reason, even to the boy who'd once stolen her cigarettes from her purse years before, at another school, at recess time.

The boy didn't know that he spoke a foreign language, didn't even know the name of the words he'd always spoken with his father; not until he looked back in his book and associated *purse* and *gasp* with the map he knew so well did he suspect that he knew things other people, grown people, didn't. The knowledge had made him confident, suddenly an adult with an adult's right to correct an erring teacher, and when the paddle started to fall it was the humiliation, not the pain that hurt him most of all.

To understand such a boy is to begin with the father. He was in his middle forties: a short, trim, muscular man with wavy black hair graying in a bar at the temples, once a hockey player in another country. To equals and superiors he was charming and co-operative, liking nothing better than drinks and a night on the town in Jacksonville or Tampa. The boy knew his father's friends, younger men from New Hampshire or Maine, French boys with the names that were all vaguely familiar. The boy was already looking for similar names in the textbooks and boxscores, on main streets and Dixie highways of all the towns they traveled through.

They had come to Florida four years earlier, settling first in Hartley and then moving to Fort Lauderdale. Each stay lasted a year while his father perfected his contacts, his English, and learned that he was temperamentally unsuited to working for other people. He'd been a furniture buyer in both towns, and once took the family with him to the summer showings in Chicago and North Carolina (the boy remembered Chicago for its hotels, the long nights in a murky room on the crisp hotel sheets while his parents were out at salesmen's parties, and his midnight walks down the corridors with day clothes over pajamas, sitting on the benches outside the elevators in order to greet his parents when they finally came up). Finally his father quit, and started a wholesaler's showroom in Fort Lauderdale. But, after one successful winter, Gene Thibidault was suddenly frozen out. His neon sign was smashed, his windows doused with paint, and his bank credit shortened. He was learning about the lines of force in Broward County. He sold again, at a loss, and went on the road for a year to build up his savings and moved the family back to the north Florida town of Hartley where the living was cheap. The boy had all but started school in Hartley, missing only the first grade—an almost fatal lateness, as it turned out.

For a winter they lived like widow and son, with T. B. Doe spending only five days a month with them, off the road. It wasn't the life his father preferred, though he was good at it, even at milking the poorest third of the nation—North Carolina to Louisiana—for a living wage. His mother took up substitute teaching, though the students complained they couldn't understand her. She'd come from Saskatchewan a long time ago, married in Montreal, then gone to Florida. It was his father who was keeping them South, while he and his mother dreamed of the North and of snow.

How his father had heard of the old airport, or when he first got the idea for starting a factory, the family never learned. Perhaps while he recuperated after a serious accident, when the boy and his mother had gone back to Canada for a spring and summer. When they returned, his father had leased an airport and signed the papers for a furniture factory.

And so they had moved from the apartment near South Street in Hartley two years before the baseball game, deep into the country to be near their airport. Airfields like this, built during the War for undefined purposes, dotted the South: an octopus of concrete hacked through cypress and live oak in that Florida geography of sand and swamp, palmetto and cactus, behind a wall of palms.

The furniture equipment was housed in the lone

standing hangar; the office and showroom in the old conning tower. The equipment—joiners, planers, saws, lathes, sewing machines and button presses—had been bought through the Citrus National Bank. The designs of Citrawood Furniture were his mother's, who'd been trained for that much at least, and the orders came from his father, still in casts and confined to a chair, who'd sold enough on approval to satisfy the bank.

For the boy there was the gift of concrete in the depths of the forest, a network of private highways leading nowhere. He was seven, he had a two-wheeler, and he explored.

They were not alone, back in the woods. During the war, there had been a barracks, a store, a gas station, a graded road leading in from the highway, even a cinema. Then the buildings had been plowed aside, and even the bulldozer lay quiet in the woods next to the spilled ruins of windows, shingles, and walls—even soup cans and movie projectors—that had fallen under the dull blade of the giant machine, now furry with rust.

Not far from where they lived that year in the woods stood the cabin of a migrant-worker family, down over the Florida Central tracks, closer to the lake where the mud never dried for six months of the year. You could scoop up that foul mud, thinking it fertile beyond belief, and plant seeds in it the way his mother had done, but nothing would ever grow. The migrants picked moss, ten cents a hundredweight, and sold it to his father among others, who rubberized it for sofa stuffing. There were seven children all strong enough to handle the metal poles and hooks to pull moss down from the cypress. The boy was a little too young and weak to help, but he was attracted to the Dowdys' cabin on those steaming days when his parents were at the factory and he was bored, or frightened of being alone.

He never did understand how many children there still were. The younger ones all looked alike—strawhaired, naked, bloated, playing in the sour purpleblack muck, even trapping minnows in the run-off waters in their front yard. The boy his age or a year older was named Broward as he'd been born in Broward County, out on a canal west of Fort Lauderdale. He was darker than the others, and thinner. He blinked and scratched, the film of dirt above his shorts was cut only where rain or sweat had washed across it. In return for the things he showed the boy—the nests of turtles and alligator eggs, the wild-cat beds, where to fish for something better than bream, what to rub on chigger bites, how to eat watermelon without a plate or a spoon and without stopping the motion or spilling juice—Frank tried to teach him about the rules of baseball, how to make figurines from plaster-of-paris and red rubber molds, the rudiments of reading, and how to speak.

The boy had worked all summer on the plaster figures, glazing and painting them and then walking to the highway to sell them at a nickel apiece to tourists who'd been beaten off the coast road by curiosity or social conscience. The boy and the Dowdy children would sit in the dust near the turn-off to Schofield's General Store and gas station, with a row of little Indian figures in Seminole dress set on an upturned orange crate.

It was April, well into summer in central Florida,

when the watermelon were at their ripest, and cheapest. At the general store the melons were piled around the gas tank, the doors, under the windows, and along the highway like boulders. Even the Coke machine outside was crammed with melons, at ten cents a giant slice. After selling a few of his Seminole dolls, the boy would buy a slice, return to the roadside and begin eating it, just the way the Dowdys had taught him.

One day, Broward Dowdy and a few of his younger brothers came up from their shacks, each with a melon slice which they'd been eating along the way. Their bellies were glistening with juice, and flies had sprung where the liquid had dropped on their feet.

Just then a large dusty car with out-of-state license plates slowed down and pulled into Schofield's drive. On the dashboard, the boy noticed, stood the plastic Jesus that also stood in the cars of his father's friends, and which the boy associated with furniture salesmen along with their open liquor bottles, their drinking as they drove, their turning to look at women on the sidewalks, and the dirty stories that anything in skirts seemed to start.

There were six people in this car: a couple in front with one small boy, an old lady and two kids in the rear. There were Kleenex boxes and sandwich wrappers along the back window ledge, and while the car was stopped the wife carried out a box full of litter. The little kids were pestering their father for slices of melon, and the man headed over to the boys, camera slung around his neck.

"Boys—this Route 401?"

"No, sir. Y'all lost 401 outside Leesburg."

"We want to see the Silver Spring—"

"Ain't fixin to, not thisaway."

The grandmother shuffled their way, followed by a girl younger than Frank.

"*Regarde-les, Henri!*" the old woman called to the man. "*Prends leur photo.*"

"*Papa—comment mangent-ils?*"

"It isn't hard to learn," said the boy. "Just got to keep your mouth full of seeds and find a way of spitting them out."

"*Papa—achètes-en pour moi.*"

"*Combien demandent-ils?*" the old lady asked her son.

"Ten cents a slice," said the boy. "It's cheaper for y'all if you buy a whole one."

"*Henri—ce garçon-là me comprend.*"

"Sure I understand," said the boy.

"*Ecoute, Henri—prends leur photo, vite.*"

"*Qu'ils sont tellement quioutes. Regarde la didinne—là.*"

"*Tais-toi, Lucille.*"

"*Mais y portent pas de caleçons, papa.*"

"They don't *own* any underpants," Frank said to the little girl, Lucille, his age. "Least, not in the summer."

The man, Henri, was walking around the orange crates where the boy had grouped his figurines. The Dowdys were standing behind them eating their watermelon. The tourist children were laughing among themselves, still pointing to the nakedness of the younger Dowdy children who regarded the tourist family curiously, as half-tamed animals might, waiting for a lump of sugar. Henri's wife had been cleaning the faces of her younger children, and passing cold Cokes around. She came running, as though her husband had called her to see a snake, or something odd. The three adults, a man with camera and two women, faced the children, and only Frank, hoping for a sale of his Seminole dolls, showed a ready smile.

"Mance," said the husband to his wife, "ce gamin-là me comprend. J'en suis sûr."

"Toi," she said to the boy, "avec les poupées-là. Que t'appelle-tu?"

"Frankie," he said.

"Sacrement!" whispered the old lady, crossing herself.

"Vite, Henri, avant qu'ils disparaîssent!"

The man wound his camera hurriedly and pointed it at the boys, who all dug deeper into their watermelon.

"Monsieur," said Frank, "est-ce qu'on doit sourire ou plutôt manger comme ça?"

The man was still looking into his camera, but his elbows dropped. The smaller Dowdys were backing away, afraid of the camera and the way the tourists spoke. "Them's Yankees," Broward tried to explain, "and that's jist Yankee-talk. Ain't that the way they talk, Frankie?"

"I don't know. I reckon it is."

"You a Yankee, ain't you?"

"I don't know. I don't reckon I am."

"Then how come you know what they're saying?"

It was a question the boy couldn't answer, not then and not two years later when he rose to correct the teacher's pronunciation.

But the tourists—they were Quebeckers from a small town outside Montreal—were even more frightened. The grandmother entered the date and time, and, as nearly as she could determine, the place, of this Visitation. All necessary to the registering of a Miracle. They bought all of Frank's Seminole dolls, not asking the prices, just stuffing his hand with all the change they had. Working in English, they arranged the Dowdy children around Frank and behind the dolls, the smaller Dowdys looking down into their slices of watermelon. Poor white trash, Florida crackers, migrant workers, nothing in their faces to indicate otherwise. But for a family from St. Jérôme, driving down for their first Florida holiday after the war, a Miracle had taken place, a flesh and blood Miracle captured on film that would make all the apparitions of the Virgin Mary, all the shrines and grottoes of Quebec, Spain, and other pious backwaters, blush in embarrassment. The old woman walked to him slowly, both arms out to frame him, to carry him as though he were already a doll, a framed portrait in oils. "*Tu n'es pas réel, je sais bien. J'ai peur de Toi, mon Ange . . .*" and she stopped short of touching him. "*Ni chair, ni sang,*" she said and bowed, making the sign of the cross, then planting a hesitant kiss on his dirty feet.

In days to come, the St. Jérôme paper would carry an account, and two Montreal papers, one English, would pick it up. The office of the Archbishop in Miami, to whom the entire incident was related two days later, took it under advisement, studied the photos, and put the whole story on the French-language bulletin supplied by the better hotels to their Quebec guests, under the heading, "*Miracle . . . ou Mirage?*" At least one traveling salesman that day in Miami, staying in the Patrician and picking up the French news with his tomato juice on the patio by the pool, drying out from the night before, read the story and thought of Gene Thibidault who lived up near Hartley, and who had a boy of seven or eight. He folded it up and gave it to Gene the next time he saw him; and when his father read it to him the boy remembered it perfectly. It became the first evidence—and all the proof he would ever need—that nothing secret and remote was ever lost in the world, was ever perfectly private.

2

About the same time as the Miracle, the boy had been learning to bicycle on the deserted concrete strips of the airport while his parents, ten Hartley lumbermen and two black seamstresses worked inside the factory.

He discovered a stream beyond the last bank of rusted lights at the end of the longest runway. Probably it had been a ditch dug by a wartime bulldozer and then abandoned. Maybe they'd tried to drain the swamps, almost succeeded in the dry season, then become disheartened when the winter rains came. Out a few feet, the water rippled around something rusty, and turtles' heads often broke the surface. The banks were lily-clogged and the scum was a lush grass-green as far out as a small current in the middle. The surface was in nervous agitation; the lily stalks walked and jerked, mysterious bubbles squeezed through the slime and burst with loud popping noises in the thick water, and minute by minute the smaller fish flopped and larger ones fretted the scum with a sudden spurt. Never had the boy seen water so alive. Even the worms he cast were nibbled before they could sink through the algae.

He'd never caught so many fish . . . bream, and the longer perch they called warmouth. He deepened his line and got nothing. Then he brought the bait closer to shore and didn't shorten it and in a few seconds the twig he'd tied as a bobber submerged and started limping away, slowly at first, then faster and more insistent. The fish was hooked; he merely had to pull it in. It was heavy, but not too lively. He hauled it up through the algae and watched closely as it squirmed on shore. The fish, if it was a fish, was a foot long, black and finless, though coated in scum, like an eel only thicker, with a blunt reptilian head. He dragged it onto the concrete, then dropped his pole and jumped on his bike. He'd done something that his father would want to see.

T. B. Doe was sitting at a card table just inside the entrance. Paper plates and stained cups had been pushed to one side, the cigarette-roller stood in the middle resting on a stack of invoices. A thick-set man with a puffy face and blondish-gray crewcut hair was sitting with him. The boy's mother stood by the filing cabinet talking to a woman much shorter with very black hair and the shadow of fuzz on her upper lip. A younger, better-dressed man in a shiny olive suit and cream-colored tie was in the wood room, walking down the aisles between the machines as though he were inspecting them. The boy caught his breath and walked to his mother's side.

"And this must be your li'l boy that you was tellin' me about," said the dark-haired woman. Up close it wasn't fuzz, just very bad skin with a row of blackheads above the line of lipstick. "Ain't he cute, though. What's his name?"

"Frankie."

"Ain't that the cutest li'l name, though?"

"This is Mrs. Lamb, dear," said his mother. "And Mr. Lamb, from the bank."

"My husband is givin' some money to your daddy," said Mrs. Lamb, "and that gentleman back yonder is my brother, Mr. Curry. Travis Curry, the lawyer?"

"Trav!" Mr. Lamb called. The lawyer hurried back from the far end, and was given a stack of papers to read. He signed, then stamped them with a pocket seal. Hands were shaken all around.

"Daddy—come see what I caught."

"What would you say to a drink?" his father asked, pulling out the bottom drawer. "Bourbon? Scotch?"

The Lambs took bourbon, the lawyer and his father scotch, his mother nothing.

"Daddy."

"Now I want you to watch this," said his father. "Son —you heard what everyone wanted?"

"Yes, sir."

"Then take the cups over to the cooler and mix the drinks." He looked across to the lawyer and banker. "Only seven years old and the best damn' bartender in

Oshacola County. Makes a damn' good dry martini, Manhattans, name it—trained him myself."

"Ain't that cute, though."

"Daddy—I caught a fish—"

"—only wish you were asking for something *harder*. But we're out of gin—"

"—it's *big*, daddy. It's the biggest fish I ever saw."

"Find out how much water they want first, son—"

So the boy made the drinks, simple straight drinks with a dash of cold water from the cooler, all the while thinking of the fish that lay at the end of the runway and the other things that swam under the scum and caused the bottom to bubble, the lilies to walk. It was a new water cooler with a ten-gallon jug on top; three squirts on the button brought a single fluttering bubble to the surface. He leaned his face on the cool solid glass, pressed his eyelids on it, then drew back enough to look through the water back into the office. He could still make out the women and the lawyer, the water reducing them all to balls or sticks in appropriate clothing.

"We're waiting, son."

The office seemed all the hotter, now, with his eyes still cool and rested, as though he'd just slept, as though the drinkers were in his dream.

"Can you see the fish now, Daddy?"

"What fish?"

"I've been *telling* you."

"Oh, all right."

The bike was just outside. When he stepped into the sun and began pedaling he realized how sweaty he'd gotten inside. Clouds boiled overhead, gray-on-gray flaring, like a pebble dropped into a muddy puddle, and thunder was rolling over the lake behind the trees.

He had dropped his pole and fish on the runway a few feet from the water's edge, but now he couldn't find it. Yet the concrete was wet, as though a truck had backed into the mud, and then gotten stuck, thrashed around, gotten out.

The pole was quickly found . . . at least its handle. He pulled it toward him, wondering how the fish could have dragged it so far. But the line was light as he pulled. And when he'd tugged it out of the shrubs and back onto the concrete, he saw the strangest, most frightening thing he'd ever seen. On his line was the same scummy black head, the mouth open enough to expose a set of nearly human teeth; the gills still heaving, but nearly all the body was gone. There was a backbone and part of a fin, and under the bones, part of its black intestines. The meat had been shredded from the bones, even the hook gleamed cleanly between the ribs. The boy was aware of the wind roaring in the giant cypress, the slapping of water he couldn't see. He was seven years old; he didn't know yet who he was, nor had he yet suffered for what he would become.

But the fish at his feet or whatever it had been, had seen the worst thing in the world, whatever that was. The boy knew now that both things existed, the unnameable fish and the thing that had eaten it, and knowing that, he felt he had seen the worst thing too.

Hartley was a southern town and the South was as foreign to him as the Canada and Europe he was always hearing about. He felt excluded by the holidays—Jeff Davis's birthday, Confederate Memorial Day, or the quiet explanation from a beloved teacher of why they couldn't celebrate Lincoln's birthday, though it appeared in red on most of the calendars—which added to the deep sense of deprivation that he felt in reading the northern school books. The smug references to playing in snow, the predicating of all nature experiments on the 40th degree of latitude. Yankee rituals like robins in spring, squirrels in autumn, the burning of leaves, ice skating and sledding. In their Yankee books, families went on picnics in the country. ("What's wrong with the beach?" he'd demanded, "don't they have an ocean? Or is snow a compensation?") He thought of snow as a kind of sticky popcorn one played in warmly and drily, for whenever it froze in the town of Hartley and the smudge pots were set out under the orange trees and the kids pulled themselves to school with frozen fingers gripping their handlebars, the teachers would assure them it couldn't snow. It was too cold for snow.

And so the boy concluded that Florida was a special case that no one in those cavernous cities up North could even write about. None of the fishing books described the thing he'd caught that day at the airport; none of them dared to talk about the giant fish and turtles he'd glimpsed through the glass-bottomed boat at Silver Springs; none of them mentioned the black-skinned people who filled the streets of Hartley and who howled from the balcony of the Palace Theater every Saturday morning.

It was autumn again, the boy's ninth autumn, and

his last as a Southerner. He'd been sitting in the yard watching the boys play football across the street and their younger sisters skip rope in the fine clay dust of the road. The porch radio was turned on loud, the camphor tree gave shade, and an old dog had settled in the yard near his feet to chew on a bone. Suddenly over the noise of the kids and the hum of a hot Florida afternoon, he heard the high-pitched whine of their factory truck turning the corner off the highway (ambush corner, the boy called it), and plowing its way faster than he'd ever seen it, only to lurch to a stop between the boy and the view of the game, partially on the grass and still in the road.

"Get inside, get, get!" his father cried, and now the boy heard a siren out on the highway, and he could tell it was turning too at ambush corner.

The boy flowed with the action, and soon it was furious; the older boys stopped in their tracks, the girls jumping rope hesitated, the hound lifted an ear and then settled back but the boy was already running up the stairs and onto the porch. The truck rammed farther onto the lawn, blocking the drive, and his parents jumped out. It was as though the dusty road were rising in a wave and the lawn had turned to water; a rebellion of nature that only the boy and his parents were fleeing. He flew into the house, into the living room which was the most protected (he'd often told himself, in the event of a hurricane, that he'd be safest crouched under the dining table just where the living room pinched to an alcove); and he was under the table when the screen door slammed and the living room door burst open.

This is my father, he told himself: my mother and father. But it was a dream to him, like a movie. His parents were acting; they had to be. "Gene, Gene! Don't do it!" his mother was screaming, and she grabbed for his father's arms, but he wrenched free. She was blocking the door, trying to keep it open.

He saw his father framed in the doorway, against the broken light of the screen, and thought, I don't know that man. He had never seen his father pursued, never seen him clumsy, never seen him terrified and desperate, clawing at the furniture to barricade the door. From deep in the dining room under the table the boy wanted to cry out, "Quick, call the police, Daddy!" but then he remembered the sirens. The police were already coming. So his father was blocking off the bad guys for a few minutes until the police could catch them in the front yard. But he'd left his wife unprotected on the porch. *Save her!* the boy again tried to scream, but he too was shaking in terror. Then from outside he heard his mother's voice, piercing his whimper, his father's gutteral straining, the frantic stacking of everything movable, "Gene, Gene—Frankie's in there. Think of Frankie. They're here. Gene, *listen*, they're here."

His father couldn't hear, not the way he was dashing around the living room, not the way the air was popping from his lips, the sweat dripping off his nose and chin. *Never mind me*, the boy thought. The Cavalry is coming, I can hear the bugles. They've got us surrounded, but we're holding out—

And then he turned, looking not to the front and his father, but to the side, and the kitchen. The dusty boots of two men stood at the doorway, and from the way their pants were stuffed inside their boot tops and the stripes ran up their side, he knew the police had gotten in the back door while his father was barring the front, and they were safe. "Yippee!" the boy yelled, and almost embraced their legs, and while that small victory still burned in his throat, the policemen moved. One bent fast and jerked the boy out by his shoulder, and stood him up by grabbing his collar and holding him a few inches off the floor, his thick wrist hard against the boy's throat. The other leveled his rifle at the desperate man who now had turned.

"That's better," he said. "Hands against the wall."

The room shuddered with the flashing red light coming in through all the windows, dull crimson, the heaving gills of a dying fish. Then the second policeman pointed his rifle at the china cabinet and flicked the row of Royal Doulton onto the floor. The china had always been packed in newspaper, first thing, each time they moved. "Hey, stop that!" he cried. "Gene! Frankie!" his mother screamed from the porch and his father sagged against the wall. "You son of a bitch," he said.

The first policeman still held the boy tight, but let him down.

"Reckon you'll come along now?"

From outside, over the throbbing of several engines, the bursts of a police radio through the dipping banks of red, his mother cried again. "Gene, what are they doing? Gene, sign it, for God's sake. It's not worth it." She pounded the living-room door, which didn't budge. The second cop looked once at the first and made a sign that the boy didn't understand. Then he walked toward the boy's father, rifle extended. The boy's eyes were covered by the policeman's hand, but he could feel the red lights.

"Gene, they're taking me away. Gene, do something!"

It sounded as though the furniture was being moved again. The trunk was slammed against the wall, chairs were being stacked, the dresser was rolled bit by bit away from the door. But the house was shaking on its pilings and there were other sounds that could only come from grown men trying to hurt. Then the racket died down; it was a regular noise, the expulsion of breath, like a cough, while another man chuckled.

"Leave off him, Billy Ray. Leave off him. He was in a cast."

"What about—"

"Now take that child out to his momma. What kind of barbarians is he going to think we are?"

The boy was turned and marched through the kitchen to where the back door was sprung open and the screen punched in. The dark-haired lady with the row of blackheads stood with other men on the back porch. From the living room the boy could hear her husband, Mr. Lamb from the bank, saying, "Well, sir, it looks like a nigger Saturday night in here. You see the grief you've brought on yourself—" and as the boy was pushed out the back through the knot of people, Mrs. Lamb was saying to her brother, the lawyer, "—and him such a fine-looking gentleman, too. That's where I feel so bad about it all."

The neighbor kids stood in the driveway, in and out

of the row of police cars with their red lights turning, climbing up and jumping out of the cab of the Thibi-dault truck. His mother stood between two policemen, each with their hats in hand, and as the boy approached he could see that she was handcuffed to the bug-smeared grill of their big Dodge truck. She leaned against the hood, and the boy could tell she wasn't seeing him or anything, any more. Her face was gray from the dust, rubbed white where she'd brushed it, and everything about her seemed out of focus to the boy.

The crowd applauded as the deputy led him from the house. He was being dragged and rolled like the bales of moss at the factory. Why were they cheering? The boy tried to smile—heroic survivor—but the policeman treated him roughly, more arsonist than victim. "How many more you got in there, Henry?" a deputy shouted from the street. Older people were lined up on the street, veiled by the dust from curious cars slowing down, and the lawn was filled with onlookers. The shaded part under the camphor trees where the boy had been sitting with the old hound dog was scattered with cars and the whole thing looked like a country auction, except for all the older men in shirtsleeves wearing deputy's badges. The officer, Henry, dropped him next to his mother in front of their truck. She reached out with her free hand and brushed his hair out of his eyes.

"Who in the name of Christ locked this woman up?" The same officer who had stopped Billy Ray in the living room had seen the woman handcuffed to the grille. All of the men milling on the lawn had handcuffs dangling from their belts, but only the uniformed men had guns. One of them quickly unlocked her, and apologized.

The other policemen were talking to the neighbors, answering their questions, good-naturedly and causing them to laugh. "Naw, he didn't have no gun," said one, "leastways we bust in on him 'fore he could git it out.

"Yeah, so me and Billy Ray—that's Officer Moffitt, he's still inside with Mr. Doe and Mr. Lamb—I'm Henry Stokes, come in from Bushnell," he was saying to an older man taking notes, "bust in the back door and took him by surprise . . . Naw, just him and the kid hiding under a table. I didn't see no guns, but that don't mean—

"Kid went peaceable. I expected some kind of fight out of him—the kid I mean—but he didn't give no trouble, you know? Like he figgered his old man was already guilty.

"Yeah—" he went on to someone else. "It was Mr. Lamb swore out the complaint. Assault with Intent, out at the old airport where he's got that factory. We follyed him here.

"—Right now it's Assault and Resisting Arrest and Trespassing. Trespassing at the airport—"

The policeman was going down the line of spectators, answering their questions, moving farther from the boy and his mother. Even through her skirts her legs seemed cold and dead, and her hand on his shoulder was heavy and still. He could hear a voice he knew, the lady-next-door's, snapping at the kids, "Quit that, hear?" and seconds later he felt the little limestones striking his arms and raining from gentle arcs on his head and pinging lightly on the truck.

After a long time people moved away from the house and driveway and the kids started other games in the street. One deputy came to his mother and told her they were ready for her inside and that he'd look after the boy while she went. Without answering, she took the boy's hand and pulled him along with her, and no one objected. Mr. Lamb and Travis Curry came out of the house and the people who still lined the yard cheered when they saw him. Mr. Lamb was smiling as he walked toward their truck.

"We'll be needing your signature now, ma'am," he said. "Seems your husband was mistaken about the agreement we signed, and he's prepared to make a settlement. I can't tell y'all how sorry I am about his mis-understanding—I reckon it's a little bit my fault, not informing you earlier—and what with your husband taking it kindly bad—"

His mother was looking at the banker, in the same blank way she'd been looking earlier. "Thief," she said.

"Ma'am?"

"Scum. Trash."

"Now, Mrs. T. B. Doe. You are a refined lady. Don't oblige me to change my mind. It's like Mr. Curry explained out at the airport, the bank was protecting the people's money by writing in an option clause to buy at the close of the second year."

"To steal."

"I'm pretending I didn't hear that. I'm pretending that a gypsy woman or a Jewess or whatever it is you are—hell, you ain't even Americans and you been leasing U. S. Government property—didn't call me what you done called me. A gypsy-Jewess that done took half the Oshacola County Police and two town marshals to restore order—

"Naw, I'll forget. All I want is your signature and I'll forget all of it. I'm fixing to drop all charges of a personal nature. From the first day you signed that agreement you became the unpaid managers of Oshacola County Development Corporation. We let you draw your own salary without interference. You should have taken all you could get, 'cause that's the last penny you're fixing to see. Now we assert our rights of ownership."

The sheriff interrupted. "You don't have to go in if you don't want to, ma'am," he said. "Your husband done signed all the copies inside. Travis has them right here."

"It's kindly hot and stuffy inside," said Billy Ray Moffitt.

"He broke all your china," said the boy. "He put the barrel of his gun on the shelf and knocked everything off."

"What did you do to my husband?"

"Convinced him to sign," said the officer.

"They were fixing to kill him," said the boy. "That's why they covered my eyes and took me out."

She looked at the banker and the lawyer, her eyes dry and hard. "Well?" she demanded, and they held the papers out, smiling at her and the boy. "I see," she said. They gave her a pen. "I see." They brought his father out to the porch, handcuffed to one officer, leaning on another. "I signed," he said. "What you wanted." His face was dark, red under his tan, but he wasn't bleeding. *My father gets dark, my mother gets white,* thought the boy. *He gets small, she gets large.* "They've taken it all," and he coughed, bent double, coughed some more, and cried.

"I see, I see," she kept repeating to no one especially, taking the pen and finally signing below the purple clot that even the boy could see was just a travesty of his father's legal signature.

Only his teacher seemed to care that they were leaving. His father had left that same night as soon as the driveway cleared and his mother had packed without talking to either of them. They threw out boxes of books and of broken china, tropical clothes and the little things that the police hadn't smashed but that wouldn't fit in their four moldy suitcases. At school the next day the boy had been surrounded by his classmates who'd all by then heard of it—"What'd your father do, Thibidault?" The sheriff was a hero of the boys in Hartley, a muscular man built on the order of Johnny Mack Brown. They'd heard that a man had been shot out at the airport and the sheriff had tracked the owner back to Hartley and singlehandedly captured him by rushing the back while Mr. Doe was shooting it out in front. "How many did he kill, Thibidault?" they demanded, and the boy was laughed at when he said there had been no guns except the deputy's and no one killed, but that the factory had been rushed by cops and taken over and his parents ordered off it, and the proof of that was that his father had been allowed to leave town after signing everything over and he was already on his way to North Carolina, and would send for them later. A week later a post card came from High Point and the next morning his mother went with the boy to school to collect the necessary transfer letter and report card. The teacher announced to the class that Frankie was moving and that everyone would miss him. Then she took down his drawings that lined the walls, and cut the top line with all the gold stars off the reading and spelling charts. Out in the hall she said that Frankie had made her teaching somehow worth it. She herself was thinking of quitting, she told his mother.

They'd been living out of boxes for a week; when they got back home his mother finished packing sheets, some clothes, a pan, the toaster, and they were finished with Florida. That afternoon they boarded the old Greyhound to Jacksonville and sometime around midnight, in that last of the Florida cities, after hours in the bus station drinking cokes, they boarded the chrome-plated bullet-shaped New York Local. The boy took the seat behind the driver and with a road map open to Route 1, traced the coming journey.

Wherever they went, bus drivers were friends and heroes, bringing news and carrying messages, making the waitresses put on lipstick and run a wet comb through their hair, making the old men tell what seemed to be dirty stories, and the boy realized that he was once again in his father's world, with the salesmen who traveled all night and depended on coffee and the jokes they could tell. It seemed to the boy that he'd learned more in two nights of staying awake with the drivers than he had from all his years in school and reading books.

They got off in High Point, North Carolina—the furniture city in the hills—and his father was there to meet them. It was Furniture Mart time and the town was jammed with buyers and salesmen from everywhere east of the Mississippi. The conventions in Chicago and High Point were cornerstones of the furniture life, the sort of thing the boy associated with the plastic statuary in the salesmen's Chryslers: all the young Tonys and Mikes who swapped stories about niggers and kikes and Miami Beach. And now, suddenly, the boy and his mother were at a convention and his father was there without a job or friends. He'd already bought a used Chevvie and he'd found a place for them in a rooming house in Thomasville ten miles away. For T. B. Doe there would be the hotel in High Point where the men with jobs drank all night and a clever man could pick up leads. He was seeing men night and day about a job, not letting on that the factory was gone, and that the money he carried in his wallet was all he had. Meanwhile they were to sit tight in Thomasville and Frank was to stay inside during the day, since he wasn't dressed for the cold and the truant officers might pick him up for not being in school.

They'd had their dishes broken that day in Hartley and his mother hadn't cooked a kitchen meal in nearly a month. They'd been eating out and the boy had acquired the childhood taste for French fries, hamburgers, Cokes and pie, and with no place to play or run a bike, he'd immediately begun to put on weight. His mother had bought new pants and a shirt at a Montgomery Ward's in Georgia while the bus was stopped; three weeks later he'd outgrown them and he was beginning to look—even to himself—like the sons of some of the older salesmen who used to visit back in Florida, the ones with older mothers who would talk of glands while their pale, moist-skinned sons wearing their fathers' cast-off white shirts and their own shiny pants, with rolls of fat like cushions on their necks and stomachs, eyes pressed into slits over their mounting cheeks, had sat with a Coke. They'd all looked alike in those days, those clumsy boys with high whining voices and adult-styled shoes, whose pockets chimed with change as they waddled. Frank had always been embarrassed when the Jackies and Herbie, Juniors, were brought over to visit—he'd gotten on his bike and sought out the neighbor kids. Now he could frighten a kid himself and his wrists were so pudgy he couldn't wear his watch and all the veins had disappeared off the tops of his hands.

And yet these idle days were among the best he'd known. He would waken to the sidewalks clogged with school kids, and he'd all but rap on the window with a kind of arrogant self-assertion. After breakfast his mother would go out and buy him drawing paper and new comics, and she'd pick up whatever local papers were available for herself. Sometimes his father would drive over from High Point to share a cup of coffee and let them in on job leads. They were looking for a buyer at Rosenbaum's in Pittsburgh; another in Buffalo; a man in New Jersey wanted someone to manage his furniture investments. Baumritter needed a man for Kentucky and Tennessee; Kroehler was looking for a Boston man. The boy thought he would like Boston, it was the f~ north. There was not a city in America the boy not like to live in except perhaps Hartley, Jackso and Tampa, and most certainly, High Point or Tho ville, North Carolina. Every name except the one t were living in filled him with wonder for the new things there were to learn. It was, as far as he could see, the main reason for living, with comics, drawing, and the nightly meal of hamburgers, French fries, Coke, and cherry pie coming in second.

Then just as suddenly as they'd arrived, they were gone. His father had wanted leads and now he had them, and he wasn't going to do any more rushing, he said. He'd learned with the factory. No more trust and no more lawyers, ever. And so it would be more motels, rooms where the boy drew dinosaurs from memory, or rooms in the worst parts of the cold black cities where flecks of snow (at last!) drifted against the blank walls of tenements, like ashes from a distant fire. Richmond, Baltimore, Philadelphia. Always interviewing while his mother wrote letters to old friends in Canada and he traced the maps from his mother's old Atlas they'd saved from Florida. On the walls of those overheated November rooms hung sentimental portraits of the Dionne Quintuplets, and his mother told frightening tales of Catholicism and old Quebec.

Each week led them closer to New York. All those towns read New York papers, heard New York radio directly ("Temperature in midtown Manhattan now 38 degrees"), and now and then, with enormous antennas, pulled in New York television on their tiny sets. New York was the legendary place that his mother feared and had never seen, but his father knew well and felt would be lucky for him. But New York was too expensive for all of them. Better to store them in Newark or Elizabeth, while he scouted the city for a job.

The boy was sleeping later and later, not knowing the day of the week any more, or if his parents would be in when he woke up. A series of landladies would bring him breakfasts, pouring cornflakes into a bowl, toasting some bread and leaving out the softened butter, and he would stroke their cats and watch every minute of television from the time it came on. They moved every week or two. The winter deepened. It snowed and melted, grew black, lingered on the north side of things. He still wasn't allowed out in the daytime; embarrassing questions might be asked. When they stayed in hotels, there'd be a paper bag on the dresser when he woke up, left by his mother, filled with fresh pastries and a Dixie cup of milk with a lid.

In the early weeks of the trip, he had gloated as they passed the rows of yellow windows in the sooty school buildings, but after Christmas he longed to learn something, however stupid, again. He'd take his chances with the kids, be pleased to be put in a school if only for a week or two. He was tired of filling notebooks with designs of cars and airplanes, drawings of animals and portraits of imaginary bearded men. He wanted more gold stars and perfect papers. Only when he saw the schoolyard fights developing (and how often their tourist rooms stood opposite an old brick school), with three or four kids pushing around a fatter one, the circling and punching near the bicycle racks that he knew so well, was he glad there'd be no school, no fights, for him that day, or week; not in that city, or that state. He'd never learn New Jersey history or the counties of Pennsylvania, all the battles that had taken place in Maryland, or the constitution of Delaware. Not having to learn the names of the new teachers and thirty classmates, only to leave them again six weeks later. The millions of possibilities he'd never convert! He looked out the windows, fed landladies' parakeets; drew maps of imaginary countries, harbors, rivers, coastlines, and lost himself in highway nets, urban sprawl, then named his cities in invented languages, devised their flags, labled the rivers and bays based on private words for water; watched them grow, and then with a cheap fountain pen dropped from a foot above, bombed them into rubble.

Then they were once again in another hotel, this time in Jersey City where the tips of Manhattan skyscrapers were faintly visible beyond the bluffs. It was the oldest hotel yet, with high-ceilinged rooms that were still overheated, cracked hexagonal tiles on the bathroom floor, spots of old tomato paste along the wall near the electric outlet. A single yellow bulb too high for changing, overhead. The smeared windows made his eyes water. It seemed to the boy that first night in Jersey City that they had come to the end of the world; the swamps and river separating them from Grand Central Station, museums, subways, the Empire State Building, the Stork

Club, Central Park, Radio City, the Yankees and the Statue of Liberty was the same intractable, impassable barrier that had doomed him always. New York was *there*, five miles away! The same network radio voices that had thrilled him in Florida were at home in those towers! He pressed his face on the windows, steaming the glass with the whispered magical names: Times Square, Flatbush, the Bronx, Fifth Avenue, Macy's, Madison Square Garden, Coney Island, Brooklyn, Waldorf-Astoria. Those names were all he knew of *America*; the rest of the country was an endless roadside that hardly existed.

Instead of a ring of keys, he was left with a single room key attached to a bulbous rubber tail—too fat to stuff in a pocket and carry away—but just right for lobbing in the air, and counting the revolutions it made before plunging down. He lay on the cot the next afternoon, studying the ceiling as though it were a floor, tossing the key upward as though it were diving. It snowed a little that day, enough to whiten the tops of cars. In the schoolyard below him, kids scraped together enough for a snowball fight before their recess ended. It had once been his dearest wish, in Florida, to play in snow. But now, the snow no longer excited him.

As he watched the melting snow outside, the idea struck him to build his own snowman. Indoors, with what he had. He'd always drawn things, never built. Afraid of cluttering things, of cutting himself. He bundled all the old papers into balls and began stuffing a shirt and pair of pants he could no longer wear. He stuffed them good and fat until the buttons were popping, then blew up a paper bag for the head and painted on the hair and features. He had no carrot for the nose, but he did have paste and more paper bags, and he blackened a gaping hole for a mouth crying out. He put mittens over the shirt cuffs and socks over the ends of the pants. It took him the better part of the day and it suddenly seemed vital to have it done before his mother got home.

He sat the model on a chair, then in bed. He thought of sitting him on the ledge outside their window to see if a crowd would gather, but the window was locked for the winter. Then, with his parents just minutes from coming, he took off his belt and looped it around the dummy's neck, and then found a place on a chandelier to hook the buckle. The dummy jerked and tightened and then swung back and forth, just so. The boy waited by the elevators, running back to the room each time the arrow started up from the lobby. He was waiting behind the door when the familiar crinkle of shopping bags and his parents' talking filled the hall. He gave the dummy one last turn as they rapped. They knocked louder and his father cursed as he put down the bags. "He must be sleeping," said his mother, and his father said, "I sure as hell hope he hasn't gone out," and his mother answered, "No, he knows not to," and his father replied: "All he does is sleep." The boy was almost hysterical with suppressed laughter and his bladder burned with sudden urgency.

The moment the door swung open, his mother screamed; sharp inhuman screams with every breath she took, that brought an opening of doors and rushing of feet down the hallway, as she sunk to the floor, and the groceries she'd dropped. Her screaming went on as his father, arms free, rushed in and pulled at the dummy's pants and they came off in a shower of paper balls, and the boy took his hands off his mouth so they could hear his hysterical giggle. "Mildred, Mildred!" his father was shouting though no one heard, and looking straight over the boy to the woman slumped in the doorway, hands—arms up to the elbow—covering her head and chest, dry breathless sobs ripping from deep inside. No one heard his laughter. The hall was jammed two and three deep with women in housedresses and men in bath-robes, some smiling, others stunned and whispering. Even the boy himself had joined his mother at the door, shaking her, saying, "Hey, it was just something I made, that's all. I thought you'd like it, I really did." His mother looked out once from behind her arms, like a child lifting his head against a blow that he knows is coming, and his father jerked him up, lifted the full hundred and thirty pounds his son had become, and shook him, shook him as though he had indeed been paper and stuffing, then threw him in the direction of the bed. "Get back, get out, get the jesushelloutofhere all of you!" he screamed, kicking the rubbish, the bottles of milk, the slices of meat for the hot plate, the broken bottles of instant coffee into the hall, laying his hands on the shoulders of men to push them further and faster so the astonished women would follow. And while his father was in the hall the boy climbed on the bed. His mother ran to him and fell across him, and the deep jerking sobs began again.

His father, returning, must have looked once, then slammed a door they couldn't hear, for he didn't come back that night, nor for several days. A week later he told them only of a blizzard that had caught him outside of Rochester. Then he mentioned he'd found a room off Broadway on 92nd Street, and they'd be moving into the city that very night.